Boyz in the Grove

by
Rick Darby

authorHOUSE™

1663 Liberty Drive, Suite 200
Bloomington, Indiana 47403
(800) 839-8640
www.AuthorHouse.com

First published by AuthorHouse 12/22/05

ISBN: 1-4259-0169-7 (sc)

Library of Congress Control Number: 2005910758

Printed in the United States of America
Bloomington, Indiana

This book is printed on acid-free paper.

Acknowledgments

So many people encouraged me during this project and I could never thank them all. There are some very special people who inspired and pushed me enough to make *The Boyz in the Grove* a reality.

My wife, Debbie, has always believed I was more than I could see myself as. She has walked every step of the way and is still right beside me. I am eternally grateful God put us together.

Then, there is the one who told me I had to write and stirred up the gift I had for years. Debbie's seventh grade school teacher, Phyllis Fountain, who came into our lives several years ago, gave me the courage to start putting these words on paper. Phyllis said these words, "Just do it, honey; it's already in you."

Debbie and I have four grown children. They always loved hearing my stories. If they had not listened even when they didn't want to, I may have never done this. To Tiffany, Andy, Melissa, and Richie, "I love you."

The greatest of all my encouragers is my Lord and Savior Jesus Christ. It all belongs to Him because He gave me the gifts and callings in my life. To Him be the glory.

Table of Contents

THE BOYZ IN THE GROVE

Preface

Memories are things that grow fonder by the year. They allow you to revisit old times. I don't guess it is real proper to say that until you've reached forty. I grew up in the rural South, just as many of you who will read this book. You may then ask, "Well, why would your story be any different than mine?" Honestly, a lot of it could be very similar. I hope this book will make you think of the sweet smell of honeysuckle or "the turn-your-mouth-inside-out taste of a pomegranate," maybe even the inviting fragrance of an ol' country outhouse. Memories of your first red wagon or the first person you kissed, besides ya mama, maybe even the mischief you found yourself in; makes you think, huh? At least that is what I hope. As you read these stories, and that whimsical grin appears, you may start some recollecting of your own....

It all starts in the Pecan Grove, not a magical place, but it may become a little mystical to you. The characters all represent folks I grew up with or remember during those good ol' days. Nobody you will read about was famous or gained any particular notoriety, some of them didn't even finish high school. I did change some of the names of my friends because they just don't need folks pestering them. They come from blue-collar families, salt-of-the-earth folks. I happen to think that was the best kind of raising. As you will see, a bunch of roughneck boys can have a REAL time. We didn't need computers or cell phones, two-way radios, or a wireless modem to communicate. We had the Pecan Grove yell and used two old vegetable cans with strings tied between 'em to communicate. We didn't have the luxury of fast food on every corner, so Mama's homemade biscuits and salmon patties and her fried taters and onions were talked about in the same vein as a Big Mac is for some of you.

Those were the days of The English Racer (a bicycle). Coke was real popular, and it was a soft drink not a drug you put up your nose. All soft drinks were Cokes to us; there were just different kinds like Sprite, Grape, and Dr. Pepper. A CD was something you used to save money or maybe an adult's initials or name. We had 45 and 33 records and phonographs, not stereos, and if you were lucky enough, you might see an eight-track tape player here and there. We never heard of karaoke, but we did pretend to be great singers and made our own microphones out of a cardboard center of used-up toilet paper.

Everybody involved in these stories could probably remember things a little differently. It may not have happened exactly like I tell it either. This is just the way I remember it, for the most part, anyway. I get to thinking sometimes about all the stuff me and the boys got into. It's a wonder we didn't ALL serve time or end up in the hospital. My mama and daddy reminded me of that from time to time, too. My daddy would tell me, "Boy, I'm surprised you ain't dead."

I had to put these thoughts on paper because my mind ain't like a steel trap anymore; it's more like a worn-out rabbit box. You are lucky when you catch it, but you are not quite sure how to get it out. This may be far too complex for some of you intellectuals to understand, so just ask someone with some country raisin' to cue you in on the details. I have always liked to tell stories and it seemed a lot of folks enjoyed hearing them. Several close friends told me that I ought to write a book. I really think they were all just tired of hearing all my stories and figured this would shut me up.

I sure fooled them, because now I am telling more stories than ever.

As this story unfolds, remember, it could very well be your town or city all this occurred in. It is my desire that you really get to know The Boyz in the Grove. I think this book will probably make you laugh, cry, embrace memories, and sometimes probably even be shocked.

I left the Pecan Grove in 1973, fresh out of high school and moved to town. I was grown and had the world by the tail. I thought I was leaving home but I was really just leaving the house. My folks never left that neighborhood. They lived in the same spot for over forty years. It was the only brick house in the Pecan Grove. They both passed on, and we sold the old home place, but memories will never grow old. Man, if walls could only talk. My only regret is somehow, over the years, not writing down some of the things that happened, from the adult's point of view. It would have been nice to know what Mama or Daddy thought or maybe Teddy and Ruby Lassiter, our next-door neighbors. I could have really gotten some ideas from John and June, Brent's parents, or Blue and Larue, Jacob and Johnny's folks. I didn't do that, though, and I surely regret it. A good many of those folks are gone now, but they certainly left some fine memories.

I moved away almost twenty years ago and things have really changed. I never see my old friends, unless somebody dies and we meet up at the funeral home. We all have gone our separate ways and done our separate things. There is no doubt in my mind, if you meet any one of them, they could tell you a story or two about growing up in the Grove.

I did meet up with an old acquaintance the other day. We were talking about living in Covington, Georgia during the sixties and seventies. He just affirmed what I already knew but had not, and will not, go in to details on, not yet anyway. He said, "Remember that movie called *Midnight in the Garden of Good and Evil?*" I told him I did. He then said, *"Some of the things me and you know about would make that movie look like a nursery rhyme. A lot of that stuff will go to our graves with us though, won't it?"* The only answer I could give him was *"Well, maybe so."*

ENJOY THE READ......

CHAPTER 1

A Most Unusual Call

It had been another hectic day at work and I was exhausted. I woke up in my old burgundy recliner just as Law and Order was rolling the credits. I looked at my wife and asked her if she was ready to turn in. We agreed it was time to get a good night's rest.

Usually, when my head hit the pillow, I was out like a light. This night was no exception. I was just about to get into that deep sleep when the stupid phone rang. I raised up and looked at the caller ID. I could barely make out Augusta. I started not to answer but I figured I had better see who it was, especially doing the kind of work I do.

"Hello," I said in the best friendly voice I could muster.

"Yes, is this Mr. Darby?" the voice on the other end of the phone asked.

I wanted to say, "No, this is The Pizza Hut, could I take your order?"

I figured whoever it was had some business with me. I said, "Yes, it is."

"Mr. Darby, this is Chaplain Greg Bryson with the Augusta Regional Medical Center. I am sorry to be calling you at this hour but this is somewhat of an emergency."

"Yes, Chaplain, what is it?"

"Mr. Darby, did you grow up in Covington, Georgia?"

"Yes, sir, I did."

"Are you familiar with a Jake Hartley?"

"Jacob Hartley from the Pecan Grove?" I asked.

Chaplain Bryson said, "I believe we are talking about the same man."

I asked the Chaplain what was going on with my old friend. He said, "Mr. Darby, Jake has been in the hospital here for about two weeks. I found out he was critical so I went to visit him. When I asked if there was anything I could get him, he said, 'Yeah, I need you to find someone.' I figured I would try and fulfill a dying man's wish, so I agreed. He told me, 'I need you to find an old friend of mine.' I thought it would be no problem. Sir, do you know how many Darbys there are in the state of Georgia?"

By this time, I was wide awake and wanted to know more. As the chaplain and I talked, I discovered Jake had cancer and was not expected to live an awful lot longer. Pneumonia had set up and my old friend was real weak. He asked me if there was any way I could take off pretty quickly and come. I told him I would make arrangements and be there by about noon the next day.

When I got off the phone, my wife, Debbie, had already turned on the lamp next to the bed. She asked me what that call was all about. I told her Jacob Hartley was dying and wanted to see me. She said, "What could he want? You hadn't seen him in almost twenty years and then it was for only a couple of hours. I've heard so many Hartley stories I feel like I know him as well as you. I am glad you are going, though."

I told her I believed the last time we had seen him was when he and his wife came to church with us back in Covington. She nodded and started to lean over and turn the lamp off when I said, "Did I ever tell you the story about when Jacob and all of us painted the town?"

She said, "Yes, honey, only about a hundred times. Now let's try and get some rest; you have got a long drive in front of you tomorrow."

She switched off the lamp and I lay back down, but as you might suspect, I didn't sleep very well. The alarm went off at 6:00 a.m. and I rolled over for another forty-five minutes or so. Debbie got on up and got ready for work. When she was heading out the door, I was headed for the shower. All I could think about was Jacob, Johnny, his brother, and some of the other roughneck boys from the Pecan Grove. Jacob really was not a very old man; he was only fifty-two. He had just had some rough times.

By about 8:30, I was getting in my car and headed for Highway 441. Commerce to Augusta was about a two-hour ride and my only prayer was that I would get to the hospital in time. I knew there would be a couple of stops to make before I got there. There were some things only Jacob would enjoy. During my travel time, I listened to Beach Boys music and pondered in my mind what Jacob would want with me.

Finally, about 10:45, I pulled into the parking lot. While finding a parking space, I was noticing the old hospital and the architecture. The only thing that was out of the ordinary was that there was a half-dozen or so Department of Corrections vans parked all around. I did see a few Crown Vics that looked somewhat official, too. I went on in to the front desk and asked for Jacob's room number. The receptionist told me he was in Room 513. I walked down the hall and boarded the elevator. As I headed up, I remembered why things looked a little more familiar. This was the same hospital my brother was in when he served his short prison term years ago.

So Jacob was in prison again. I wondered what had happened. I got off the elevator on the fifth floor and was quickly greeted by two strapping corrections officers and a metal detector. I had a small brown bag with my surprise for Jacob. Of course, the guards had to check it before I could go very far. When they started to hand it back, they said, "You must know him better than we do." Then they said to me, "You must be Mr. Darby."

I looked at those boys and said, "Now, how did you know that?"

One of the guards said, "We were told you were coming, and to be honest, these patients don't get that many visitors. Follow me, sir, I will take you to Mr. Hartley's room."

We walked down the hall and I could just sense that there had been some rough characters up in this place. We stopped and started to turn left into the room when the guard spouted, "Hartley, you've got a visitor."

I walked into the doorway and looked at an old frail body lying in the bed. There was no way I could have ever recognized him. His white hair was thin and his face was sunk in and his gray moustache was stained from all the smoking over the years. He looked at me and tried to adjust those dull blue eyes.

"Who are you?" he asked.

"Darby's the name, Rick Darby."

Jacob lit up like you had pumped energy into his veins. "Man, you can't believe how happy I am to see you. How you been, boy?" As the big lump came up in my throat, I told him I had been doing great. When I got a little closer to the bed, I could see the IV, catheter, and the oxygen.

"Sit down, Darby, you ain't got nowhere you got to be, do you?"

I pulled the straight chair up next to the bed, and before I sat down, Hartley was telling me he didn't want me to know he was in prison again. He said, "I figured if you knew

I was locked up, you wouldn't come. It is real good to see you, though."

Hartley looked at me and said, "You know, it's been thirty-four years this month."

"I know, Jacob, but I didn't come here to talk about all that," I told him.

"No, no, I don't either; I just was thinking and wondered if you remembered."

I just told him there would be no way I could ever forget April 1971. I handed him the paper bag. "Just thought you would appreciate this."

He opened the sack and pulled out a couple of Stuart pecans. "I guess that's to remind me where I came from," he said with a little crooked grin. Then he reached inside and pulled out a can of orange spray paint. I asked him if he remembered orange spray paint. "You bet your ass I do, my elbows still ain't the same." After the paint was a pine sapling. He looked kind of puzzled. I told him I would explain it later. Then I gave him a CD that I thought I would never find. It was from Credence Clearwater Revival. Now, that got him real excited and he reminded me that this was his favorite group ever.

Darby, "How's ya mama 'n 'em?"

I tried to bring him up to date over the past twenty years. I asked him if his folks were still living. He said, "Daddy is eighty-two and he still gets around——Mama is eighty. They just can't travel anymore."

We both agreed family was important, and it got me to thinkin' about how it was when we were growin' up and folks started asking about our families....

5

CHAPTER 2

Who's Ya Mama 'N 'Em?

It's odd to me that every time an adult meets someone much younger, they always want to know who you are kin to. The ol' timers would say, "What's your name, boy?"

"I am Ricky Darby" would be my sincere reply.

"Are you Bud Darby's boy?"

"No, sir, J.B. Darby is my daddy."

Next, I would hear, "Is he the one that lives on Jackson Highway or does he work at Cohen's Department Store?"

It never ended there, though. The quizzing went on and on and on. "Larry your brother?" Once they figured who you were, they had to climb the family tree and mine had plenty of branches. "How are you kin to the Darbys on Collum Road? The Darbys on the other side of Porterdale— are they the same set?" I expect you know exactly what I'm talking about. You almost had to pack a lunch just telling about your family.

"Mama 'n 'em" was a term of endearment in our neck of the woods. You would hear statements like, "How's ya mama 'n 'em?" Or maybe when asked where you were going, your reply would be, "We're goin' over to Mama and ' n 'em's for supper. So I guess it's time we get to know not only my mama 'n 'em but some of the other families in the Pecan Grove, too.

My mama's name was Christine Grace Darby. Everybody knew her as Christine, but as you might guess, I called her

Mama. From what I know, she never lived anywhere but Covington. Her daddy left before she was ever born. She did try to find him one time, though. There was a lot more to that story, but I don't know it and right now, it is not that important. What I do know is my granny was one of the finest Christian women that ever walked the face of this earth. She ended up working extra hard just to support her family. She found a job in the cotton mill. They lived right there in the mill village so Granny could just walk to work.

Covington Mill was a thriving area at that time. There was the company store, the Covington Mill School, and even a couple of churches. Calvary Baptist was one of them and Granny called Calvary home.

She married two more times after her first husband left her. Her next husband gave her three more children, two boys and a girl. He passed away fairly young. If I have my facts straight, he had a heart attack. Then she married Loy Skelton, who had children from a previous marriage. He was a rounder at first. He loved his liquor and had a foul mouth, but if anybody could tame him, my granny could. She did just that, helped him get his life straight, he joined the church and went to Sunday school every week for twenty-five years. Granny faired real well; she raised a Baptist preacher, a Delta executive, and a regional manager for Sears-Roebuck.

Besides Mama, there was one more daughter who pretty much raised her young-uns on her own and held down a job at Woolworth's until that place folded. Aunt Helen was a strong woman. She had lived with an alcoholic husband, who lost his life tragically. Sometimes, I think she was better off.

Now my mama was no slouch when it came to home-cookin'. Thursday night was always fresh biscuits, salmon patties, and English peas. Fresh vegetables were FINE when

Mama fixed 'em. She might smell up the house with those collard greens, but, man, it was worth it. She would always let me crumble some cornbread in the pot-liquor and eat it when the greens got low.

There were four of us and I was the youngest. It started with Linda, Carolyn was next, then Larry, who was nine years older than me. My sisters were old enough to take care of me when I was little and what I hear is that they spoiled me rotten. Both of them were real pretty, too. The word was Linda had a mean streak in her, though.

As you already heard, my daddy was J.B. Don't ask me what J.B. stands for, because I don't know. Linda said she knew, but it just ain't that important anymore since all I ever heard was J.B. Daddy didn't have a fine education; he just finished sixth grade. He had to quit school and work to help raise the family because he was the oldest, too. He had a brother named Earnest, aka Bud, and Daisy was his sister. His papa did some sharecroppin' and worked around a farm when they were all growin' up.

Quitting school didn't keep him from being a smart man, though. He could figure out about anything. I remember him liking numbers so he was always piddling on a scratch pad; there were no calculators then. If Daddy could have done anything, he would have probably been a doctor. I think he had that in him because of the time he spent in the hospital and clinic during the war.

He got drafted in the forties right after he and Mama got married. That was during WWII. He never saw any war time, though. While he was still in the States, he got two of his fingers cut off somehow. I never knew what really happened there, either. What I do know is that he was terribly homesick and had never left the States. I guess I heard a half-dozen stories about how that accident happened but never was clear on it. He did spend eight months at the Army clinic in Texas. Anyway, the best I could get is that it had something to do with a campfire and an axe. Those two missing fingers never slowed him down, though. His little brother, Bud, served time in the Army, too. He ended up with a Purple Heart. If Daisy had gone, she would have probably whipped half the enemy barehanded. Word was she could scrap with the best of them.

Daddy was a hard worker and a good provider for his family. He worked at the Atlanta Army Depot in Conley for twenty-five years. He worked part-time at the A&P Grocery Store, too. He had a bad habit, though; he would tell you just the way it was. He may have written, "You can take this job and shove it," because that is what he would tell his bosses in no uncertain terms. Sometimes, his language got quite colorful. He could get real descriptive with the four-letter words. I looked some up in the dictionary but could never find them. Somebody told me something about Daddy being able to "cuss like a sailor." That did confuse me a bit, because Daddy was in the Army.

I can't remember him ever having any hair; I thought for the longest time he was born that way. From what I understand, at one time, he did have beautiful, wavy hair and the women loved it. My mama didn't fall for all his stuff, though; she stood him up on their first date. They had met at an old skating rink. Daddy was supposed to be a real good skater. Anyway, after some courting, they got hitched on their favorite covered bridge. They were married for over fifty years.

Daddy would have never been in *Vogue* magazine but he could have made *The Farmer's Almanac* with his old ragged jeans, a holey T-shirt, brown lace-up boots, unlaced, and a plug of Bull of the Woods chewing tobacco. J.B. Darby was a real sport model.

On one side of us, in the only two-story house in the Pecan Grove, was Teddy and Ruby Lassiter. Their house was always pretty, too. That fresh white paint and the green shutters with a nice big manicured lawn just made it look like a show place. Teddy worked for the gas company, where he drove a delivery truck. Ruby worked, too. She helped run Lang's Restaurant on Jackson Lake. They eventually bought the place from the Langs. They seemed fairly well off. One reason I thought that was because they were the only ones in the neighborhood that had a maid. I could tell you a lot more but I need to move on. The one thing I do remember was Ruby died as a real young woman. The rumor was she had a bad drinking problem. All I know is she was always good to me. I tell you, when she died, it about tore Teddy up. He got to drinking so bad we were afraid somebody would find him dead.

Next door to the Lassiters was my best buddy, Brent Mask. John and June were good people. John was the epitome of the Southern dad. When you saw him, he had a cigarette in his mouth, an old pair of khaki jeans, a flannel shirt, and dirty work boots. They had a nice place there and he was always raising birds or chickens. One time, he raised quail and Brent had an incubator under his bed. He loved to hunt and fish, too. I remember him even catching snapping turtles. Now, Brent and I were the founders of the Pecan Grove yell. I can't describe how it sounded; you would just have to hear it. The rest of the boys picked it up from us. The Masks even pulled a little trailer in the yard so his granny would be close by. Brent was the only child until he was eight or ten years old. He had a little brother come along; they named him Chris. Brent and I spent most of our waking moments together between the ages of six and fourteen. He was a year younger and a little bigger, too. What I mean is, I was skinny as a bean pole and Brent had a little meat on his bones.

There were Bruno and Sylvia Smith, our other next-door neighbors on the other side. They ended up selling the house to Ronnie and Carolyn O'Kelly. The two men had a parts store in Conyers at one time. Ronnie had a '60 Chevrolet Impala with a 409 engine. They were a real neat couple and had two girls after they moved there. Next door to them were the Warrens. Oscar and Mary Warren had two sons around Linda and Carolyn's age. Their grandsons were about our age. I heard a story about Linda hitting Sammy Warren in the mouth one time, 'bout turned him slap around. I told you she was a scrapper, didn't I? The Hartleys lived next to the Warrens. Then there were the Shrouds. Johnny, Joe, and Mary Ann were the three children. Johnny and Joe were older but Mary Ann was a year younger than me.

I know there is a lot more that could be told about these families, but I just tried to give you a little snapshot of the Pecan Grove.

BACK AT THE HOSTITAL

Jacob said to me, "You ain't changed a bit, boy. Get a chance to tell a story and you jump on it with both feet. It used to drive me crazy when we were kids but I knew your old silly stories would bring me a little peace. I want you to know I have made it right with my maker, though."

"I have prayed for you for years, Jacob. That makes me feel real good," I told him.

"I GOT TO HEAR THE ONE ABOUT THE RED WAGON" —JACOB HARTLEY....

CHAPTER 3

The Runaway and the Red Wagon

Things have to get pretty rough to make the kind of decision I was about to make. I had had enough. It was time to put up or shut up. After all, a man's gotta do what a man's gotta do. You may not realize it, but life is hard. Sometimes, if you don't see eye to eye, then you just got to cut your losses and move on. I know you have felt the same way from time to time. Listen, all is fair in love and war but........Well, you know a man's gotta do what a man's gotta do.

I might have only been five, but I was a mature five years old and I was big for my age. You know, at this point, it even escapes me why I had come to the boiling point, but I'm sure it had great validity. What really got my goat was that my mama told me it would be alright if I ran away from home, the very nerve of her. Was her brain out to lunch or what? My mind was made up, though, I was leaving and no one would stop me. I didn't even think I might need some money for my trip; food didn't come to mind, either. You know, since I was leaving and all, the least Mama could have done was pack me some sandwiches and Kool-aid. But nooo, she just said for me to go on if I was leaving. I remember she said something about me not getting far anyway. For the life of me, I couldn't figure out why she was no more concerned than she was.

If that was what they wanted, then leaving was what I would do. I went into my room, got two pairs of Fruit of the Loom underwear, my white socks with the red and white stripes at the top, and my stuffed brown puppy. I put them in a great big wrinkled brown grocery sack and out the door I went. I needed a mode of travel; after a while, my extensive wardrobe would grow heavy and I could go no further. As I scanned the vast open space of the new frontier, aka, the back yard, I saw the logical choice: my big red Western Flyer wagon. The solid rubber tires and that wooden-stake body along with the smooth pulling power made it perfect. I stuffed my clothes in and my wayward journey began.

As I began to pull my wagon through the back yard, I came up with the perfect idea. I'd hide out at Earnest and Mammy's until I could figure out where I would go. Earnest and Mammy were a couple of old black sharecroppers that lived back of the house in a dilapidated two-room shack. All the kids around loved them both. Some of the older kids would walk with us to their house. It never failed when we went, Mammy would have fresh lard biscuits she had cooked in her coal stove. We would always sit on the porch and they would tell us stories that never got boring and were better than listening to the radio. I just knew if anybody would understand my plight, Earnest and Mammy could. After all, they had experienced hardship and rejection themselves.

As I left the yard and pulled my wagon toward the narrow red-clay road, I got to thinkin'. Earnest and Mammy lived a long way from home (about 500 yards). I didn't think they had a television or radio either and of course, they didn't have videos cause none of that had been invented yet. As neat as it seemed when we visited, I suddenly remembered two more things: *They ain't got running water or electricity. Earnest don't even own a car.* Home was already looking better to me. I was not gonna watch Officer Don and the

Popeye Club or Roy Rogers on TV at their house. I couldn't sit in front of a window fan there, either. The only coolin' off I would see at Earnest and Mammy's was from the old funeral home fans.

Mama had always taught us the ways of the Good Book. Of course, I was no scholar or anything but I could remember a few things. She always said, "You supposed honor your father and mother," and <u>I was not doin' that very well.</u> She told me if I got mad at somebody, "You ought to always forgive them." I did know Mama was a wise woman. No, I was not weak and caving in, I must have just overreacted. Now, don't you go get that grin on your face like that 'cause you done the same thing plenty of times, I'm sure.

They (Mama and Daddy) had done me real wrong, but if I was gonna follow the Good Book, I had better suck it up and take it like a man. I had probably taught them a lesson anyway. As long as I had been gone, they had to be worried sick. I remember anytime anybody was gone fifteen minutes like I was, I knew how people would panic, I had already seen it. When my brother was in the bathroom over ten or fifteen minutes, my dad would say. "You alright in there, boy, or do I need to throw some rope in?"

As I pulled my Western Flyer back in the yard, I heard my mamma calling. "Ricky, come on in; supper is on the table." I left everything right where I had laid it in that red wagon and took off like greased lightning.

As I pulled up to my place, Daddy said, "You want to ask the blessing, Son?"

That day added extra meaning to: "God is good, God is great, let us thank him for our food, Amen. Oh yeah, God, thanks for such good mamas and daddies, too."

BACK AT THE HOSPITAL....

Jacob's eyelids were touching each other every few seconds. He looked up once more and said, "Earnest and Mammy loved us boys, didn't they? I wish I could tell them how much they helped me. I don't guess that will ever happen, unless I see 'em in Heaven."

CHAPTER 4

Some Things a Boy Just Never Forgets

Everybody says a child learns more between the ages of three and six than any other time in their lives. That may well be true but a boy can really learn about people between seven and nine. Some folks you just never forget, and yes, there are those you wish you could.

Earnest and Mammy were two that I still think about every once in a while, even over forty years later. What is it that makes me remember them and what they did? Besides some of my neighbors and friends, there is not much I can say about the early sixties unless I think so hard it makes me dizzy. I don't remember who the president was. I can't remember what music I liked. I don't even remember how many girlfriends I had. (It could be that I don't remember how many girlfriends because there were none.)

When I think about riding my twenty-inch red bicycle with the banana seat back to where this sweet couple lived, there are still so many things that flood through my mind. There was a time I spooked my first covey of quail and it 'bout scared me to death. The sweet aroma of honeysuckle nestled in a thicket of briars that had blackberries on it. I won't ever forget those wild scuppernongs and those pretty little wild roses. I used to eat those grapes right off the vine;

17

those things were some kind of good. One of the sweetest smells was that of the old couple's outhouse. It wasn't the kind of sweet you might think about. To be honest, it stunk; I mean, after all, it was somebody else's crap and pee. It just made us remember where we were and reminded us sometimes the simple things are better.

There was just something about those two, and at first, I couldn't quite put my finger on it, but now I believe I can. It is described in one word, but I can't reveal the word until I explain it to you. This is not a word a seven-year-old boy had any business using. It just didn't fit his vocabulary. Besides, my mama and daddy never heard it and might accuse me of coming up with a new cussword or something. The word should only be used by the scholarly and highly intelligent. Yes, that does leave me out, but let me splurge at least this one time. Every time we visited Earnest and Mammy, they had a kind word for us and treated us as their own. In the midst of desegregation and bigotry, they never noticed their skin color was different than ours. They never mentioned anybody calling them names and treating them any differently. They never complained about living in an old clapboard house that had never seen a coat of paint. Modern conveniences we could not live without didn't concern them at all. They were content with just having two rooms; that's all they needed anyway. Earnest even hauled his water from an old well, but we never heard a sigh. He was called a sharecropper and helped the Cook family who owned about five hundred acres around there. Paul Cook was a highfaluting lawyer in town and a real powerful man.

Anyway, Earnest and Mammy were both already up in age when all the kids met them, probably in their mid-sixties and believe me, that was old to a seven-year-old. That didn't stop us, though. We always loved seeing them. Earnest always kept a big yard cut but didn't have a gas mower. He had a big garden but didn't have a tractor. He told us about how he had used a mule to plow the cotton fields.

Now, Mammy, she was different from anybody I had met up to that time. She would call me "honey child" and "sweetness." We would stand in the yard while she sat on that creaky porch in an ol' cane rocker. She would tell us stories that would outdo any television show I had ever seen. It was kinda like having Uncle Remus or Mark Twain right close by. Sometimes, she would send a wild rose home to give to our mamas. "Tell everybody Mammy loves 'em, sweet boy." It never failed her asking us about our family. Mammy had a family Bible but couldn't read or write. I guess others read to her, but she still knew an awful lot about the Good Book. She would tell us about how she loved God and was looking forward to goin' home one day. Her real home had a mansion with her name on it and she was gonna walk on streets of gold. I didn't understand that at the time, because I thought she was already home. She would say, "I am gonna be with my precious Jesus one day."

In a nutshell, they knew what love was. This is not something everybody understands or knows how to share, but they did. Here comes that fifty-nine-dollar word: *agape.* Right, you may say, so you are in over your head now. No way are you going to get out of this one. Hold on, before you start judging my intelligence now, let me try and redeem myself. *Agape* is a word that I discovered later in life, a word that proved there is an unconditional love, one that never boasts, condemns, or seeks it's own. This is a love that keeps no account of wrong; it is gentle and kind. A kind of love we could sure use today. That was what an old sharecroppin' couple showed me whether I deserved it or not. It would be nice if we could find more Earnests and Mammies in the world, now wouldn't it? Reckon most of 'em like that have done died out.

You could probably close your eyes and remember some of those old saints that made you feel the same as my old sharecropper friends. It wouldn't hurt just to stop and go back even if it is just for a minute or two.

You know, as my thoughts and memories date back to those good ol' days, there is somebody else I need to tell you about. Just follow along with me as this story begins.

A lot of times, when you are the youngest, it means you will be treated differently. That was my case because all my siblings were at least nine years older than me. When I was seven, my older brother, Larry, was sixteen. My two sisters were already grown. Mama never said I was an accident but a slipup may better categorize it. I hear in those days the best birth control a woman could use was Bayer aspirin. If she just held it firmly between her legs, there was no way she would get pregnant. I guess Mama either never heard about that or Daddy put a stop to it.

I tell you one thing, though, my brother Larry was mean as a snake and loved playing practical jokes on everybody. I remember he was always up to some kind of mischief. He was cool, though, with them penny loafers and his blue jeans rolled up. He kept his hair cut in a flat-top with that slick Brilcream hair gel and was lean and tough.

I've got to be honest with you, I worshiped the ground he walked on. The sun rose and set on Larry Darby, at least in my eyes. He was my idol. He had this English Racer 3 speed bicycle and he could do some show-nuff tricks on that bike. I don't guess I will ever forget him sliding that thing up next to the house and leaving it lying right there on the ground. Sometimes, he would cut up some cardboard and clothes-pin it in his spokes. That transformed an English Racer to a roaring motorcycle. One day, he pulled the meanest trick in the book. He turned the bike upside down and started pedaling it with his hands as fast as he could make it go. Then he took a couple of my fingers and rammed 'em in the spokes on the back wheel. He said he wanted to see if my fingers would sound anything like the cardboard. I thought he had cut off my fingers. (By the way, they didn't sound anything like the cardboard, but my scream did sound a lot like a siren.) Needless to say, when Daddy found out, my brother had to sit on a cushion for a while. Daddy believed the Bible way, spare the rod, spoil the child, so tanning our hides was not uncommon. When Daddy got a hold to Larry, you could hear him cussing all over the neighborhood.

Well, even though Larry treated me pretty mean sometimes, I still wanted to be around him. Like me, he had a few friends around the neighborhood. I don't remember much about Johnny Shroud and Idous Lawson but I do remember Wayne Reynolds. He lived in the city and was my brother's best friend in the whole world. Sometimes, Wayne would ride his motor scooter to the house. He would end up taking me for a spin around the yard and sometimes up and down the dirt road behind the house. Now that was really something else.

Not many in the family were very athletic, but Larry had tried out for football and was accepted. I say not many, Linda could have made the girls wrestling team but they didn't have one. Larry became a Newton Ram football player. The Rams were the team to beat and my brother was one of the boys in the 1960s. Tim Christian was another star player, who went on to Auburn and ended up coaching there. I believe one of those Tarkenton boys played during those days, too. Anyway, we went to all the home football games and I could stand beside the football players from time to time. That was an honor to a young impressionable boy like me. Football was a way of life in Covington, Georgia during that time and the topic of conversation at the local drugstore every week.

Evans Drugstore was on one side of the square and Peoples Drugs was on the other. Monday morning and even up to lunch, you could go to either place and get a play-by-play.

I know there were things teenage boys didn't tell because they had a reputation to uphold. One of those secrets was that Larry and I shared a room and a full-sized bed. Our house had three bedrooms and one bedroom was for the girls, one bedroom was for the boys, and the bedroom with a half-bath was for my parents. Larry probably told very few folks he slept in a bed with a snotty-nosed young un'. When he came home, though, it really didn't seem to bother him. He would always keep me from being afraid. A dark room bothered me, unless I knew somebody was there to protect me. Larry even bought me a little floppy-eared, brown stuffed puppy. He told me when he wasn't there to hug the puppy tight and it would protect me. Somehow, I believed him and it worked. (Maybe that will give you a "warm fuzzy" or even make a lump in your throat.) Listen, it was a special thing to a boy my age and I ain't ashamed to tell it.

There is a lot more I could tell you about my brother but I figure you can relate to what you have heard so far. A year or two later, Larry had a girlfriend and he usually used Daddy's '55 Chevy to take her out. Her name was Beth Staugh and she lived down Jackson Highway close to the old Heard Mixon School. From what I could gather, she was the prettiest girl between the Boy Scout Camp and Potts Store. I remember when it finally worked out so he could get his own car. I won't ever forget the day Larry drove up in his 1957 Ford Fairlane. It was solid black with a good-looking set of hubcaps and shiny white walls. I might have been young, but I knew my cars. I tell you all this because once he got that car, we saw less and less of him. He was capturing freedom.

Sometimes, Daddy would dig around and find things in Larry's car like a pack of Swisher sweet cigars or an empty PBR beer can. Ain't it weird how none of those things ever belonged to him? It is hard to believe he would let people leave that kind of stuff in his car. As much as I fought it, my brother was slippin' away. The love bug had bit him and he was growin' up.

One day, my hero would leave, and I couldn't figure out what I was gonna do. I would cry and beg but it just didn't seem to help. Mama would tell me, she and daddy were there for me but that was different; they slept in their own bed. Larry ended up marrying his high school sweetheart and I was quite jealous about that. Finally, I just gave in and figured life must go on. Well, really, I pitched a fit about the whole thing. Even though he started a new family, I was still his only brother and that had to carry some weight...

BACK IN AUGUSTA

Jake looked at me and said, "I just wish somebody had thought that much of me. I really got my life screwed up, though." Just as he was finishing his sentence, Johnny, his younger brother, peeked his head in the room. Johnny told Jacob that there was a time he idolized him. He said things started changing in 1971.

Johnny came over and shook my hand. "Long time, no see, Rick. How have you been?" I told him it had probably been almost thirty years. Johnny had always been Jacob's little brother. It was different now. What used to be a dirty blond, curly-haired boy with ruddy skin and long skinny legs was a weathered gray-haired man with a splotchy beard. Johnny asked me, "So what brings you here after so long?"

Before I could answer, Jacob piped in and said he had sent for me through the chaplain. Jacob told Johnny I had been telling some of those old stories about us.

I pulled the pine sapling out of the brown bag and asked the two of them if they remembered our fancy forts. The sapling represented a Pine-Tree Penthouse....

CHAPTER 5

Red-clay Condos and Pine-tree Penthouses

Too many things today keep a boy busy and forbid him from discovering life's treasures. As a young boy, I never even heard of a computer or video games. The closest thing to a video game was the pinball machine at the pool hall and that place was off limits to me. Instead of Nintendo, I had a Barlow. In case you are not up on fine cutlery, that was a cheap pocket knife.

Nothing kept the boys in my neighborhood cooped in the house. We were kind of like the U.S. Postal Service. Neither rain, nor snow, hail nor storm would keep us in. Of course, Mama's hickory would discourage us from time to time, but if we could always be outdoors, we would find a way.

We had names for certain places we would meet. Some of these places should be on the national registry, but you know how the government is. We would meet at places like "the rock," "the forked tree," "the foot of the creek," or "behind the double terrace." There was something about the woods behind the Pecan Grove that just drew us in. I can't describe it but it was almost magical.

Now, let me tell you about the gang before I go any further. There was my best friend, Brent, who lived two houses up from me. He lived next door to Teddy and Ruby

Lassiter. Brent was a year younger and a little heavier with dark, wavy hair. Of course, almost everybody was heavier than me because I was skinny as a rail. Then there was Jacob, he was really the leader of the gang because he was two years older than the rest of us. He lived three houses in the opposite direction from Brent. They lived in the only blue house in the neighborhood. I guess they painted it that way to match his daddy's nickname. Jacob was a little taller, had a cool wave in his deep brown hair, and just looked kinda tough. He had a younger brother named Johnny who was somewhat of a wormy boy but we let him come along mostly because he was Jacob's brother. He was not over seven when we all hooked up. There would be others from time to time, but these boys really didn't qualify at the time because they didn't live in the Pecan Grove. If I remember, I was about nine by the time our gang was organized.

As you know, all of Georgia just ain't the same. South Georgia has gray sand and a lot of flat land. North Georgia has a lot of rocks, red clay, and hills. Where I lived, there were plenty of red clay and pine trees. This kind of thing was what a boy lived for and a mama screamed about. Mama would say, "Don't you get no red mud on them new blue jeans, 'cause you know it won't wash out." I appreciated her concern, but she just didn't have a clue what we needed to do. I mean these boys were all about building the highest quality structure possible. You are just going to get dirty when you are a part of such an important venture.

Before we began to undertake one of these projects, we had to have tools. Our personal resources were limited. I think we might have had a mattock, maybe a broken shovel, and one ax that the head kept coming off of. We all could get the tools we needed if we could sneak them away and get 'em back without daddy knowing. John Mask, Brent's pop had some pretty good tools in the old shed out back; they were just hard to sneak out. It would have been good to have a square and level but none of us knew how to use them.

Let me get you started on one of those luxurious red-clay condos. We would find a big, red-clay mound that didn't look real rocky. The first we built were in areas others could see, if they took an afternoon stroll through the woods. After all, not many people had seen the kind of workmanship we provided. We would begin by digging into the side of the dirt bank. The intent was to have three walls of red clay. We could cut down on material that way. At first, we wanted to dig down five or six feet, but I'll just say we changed our minds. (I don't know if you have tried to dig through red clay or not but it is kinda tough.) We made a makeshift yardstick out of a pine sapling and when it was level with the ground, we quit digging. Our next step was to make a roof that didn't leak. We never mastered that. Building materials were in high demand so we pretty much improvised. What I really mean is, we cut most of our own lumber. We didn't have a sawmill or a chainsaw, so you guessed it, limbs, branches, and trees we could chop and pull. You won't see any today, but our huts looked a lot like a monster. It was a huge brown and green porcupine with a red belly. Spooky, ain't it?

I forgot to tell you, but by the time we started building, both Earnest and Mammy had gone on to meet Jesus. It was never the same without them. There were a lot of old outbuildings where they lived. Earnest had a shed for every purpose. We didn't want 'em to fall down and not be used for something. (But when they were gone, nobody ever moved back in the old house.) The boys all agreed we could use some of that old wood to make us some real serious tree houses, commonly known as pine-tree penthouses. (It is better to get forgiveness than permission sometimes, I guess.)

If you built these today, they would probably have an email address and a webpage. They were fancy, for their time. We had one with three stories. It was the first high-rise in the Pecan Grove. It had ladders to each level. The décor was nothing to laugh about either. On the second level, we had several pin-ups from some girly magazines we had confiscated.

We found four pine trees close enough to make a room on each level about eight by ten. We made all sorts of plans there. That was the place we all learned to smoke, cuss, and tell lies. We all had plans to bring a girl to the tree house and have our way. We all learned to inhale right there in our penthouse. There was not much we didn't smoke either. Good thing we had not heard about marijuana. We did smoke some weed, though, rabbit tobacco along with banana peels and plain newspaper as well as recycled cigarettes. Sometimes, the place looked like a gambling parlor with all that smoke coming from between the walls. We never wanted to get caught by our parents, though. We would chew on fresh pine needles and then rub them on our clothes. It didn't work, though; we just smelled like a Pine-Sol cigarette. My daddy did walk up on me and Johnny one day, though. Blue, Johnny's daddy, made him smoke three or four big cigars and chew some Bull of the Woods chewing tobacco. It didn't phase Johnny one bit. He just blew smoke rings and had a spitting contest with his daddy.

Oh yeah, let me get back to the subject of girls. There was one problem with that, well maybe two. The first was, none of us was really sure what having your way meant. The bigger problem was that there were no girls our age in the neighborhood.

Most of the wood has rotted now and almost all of the pine trees were cut and used for timber. There were so many things we all did together; it would take years to tell it all. One thing we did learn, though, we learned that tree houses and huts fall in or rot away but memories, however faded, live a lifetime.

BACK IN JACOB'S ROOM

Jacob and Johnny just looked at each other and shook their heads. It was like they hadn't mentioned any of this in years. Then one of the corrections officers stuck his head in the room and said to Jacob, "This must be the man you have been telling us about."

"Yeah, Sarge, this is Rick Darby," Jacob replied. "Is there any way you can stay a few minutes and hear one of these stories?" Sergeant Andrew Crane said, "Sir, I would like to hear your story. I've only heard about 'em a thousand times."

I looked at my small audience and said, "Anybody afraid of ghosts?"

CHAPTER 6

I Ain't Afraid of No Ghost

The Twilight Zone, The Outer Limits, and *Alfred Hitchcock's Mystery Theatre* were just a few of the scary programs I watched on Mama and Daddy's black-and-white television. It was real hard to be in the room alone during these shows. I can remember the hair on the back of my neck standing up. I had heard all sorts of stories about ghosts and haints. Most of those stories had been passed down for years. Honestly though, about everybody I knew believed in some sort of strange phenomena. There was a family that lived down the Starsville Highway who believed their house might be haunted. That was only a stone's throw from the Pecan Grove, too. Other people in the High Point Community believed they had seen UFOs. All of us boys had heard the wildest stories ever. We had sat around the campfire and seen who could spit the furthest, yell the loudest, and scare the others the most. You know how your imagination wonders when you hear or see things that just don't seem right. Things like the headless man or the rabid wolves...You know what I mean?

Earnest and Mammy had been gone a couple of years now, but we still went down to the house a good bit. Unfortunately, we were not the only ones hanging around the old house. There were outsiders, (I mean folks that didn't live in the

Pecan Grove) who came for different reasons. They didn't have the same respect and honor as we did. These boys knew how to tear up rip. Most of the windows had been broken out and there were holes in the old, unpainted sheetrock but there was something mystical about that place still. Sometimes, I would just walk around the house and look. It was like we always expected to see or hear something. It's like when you creep around just expecting something to jump out around the corner. I reckon I had a feeling it might be haunted. Almost every time I went to the house, I would peep around the corner to make sure there was no ghost or anything like it. It is better to be safe than sorry, after all.

There was this one day, I was out gallivanting, and just like any other day, I had my pellet rifle. I had been checkin' my rabbit boxes when I decided I would walk on down to the old house. This would be a day I would never forget. As I crept up, I was thinking I might jump a rabbit or spot a deer. I heard something up around the chimney. When I looked up...I about peed in my pants. There was something I had never before seen in my life. It was some sort of huge dark bird. It looked a lot like one of those pre-historic vultures I had seen on television. This time, it was in real life. I was terrified and froze in my tracks, but I knew I had to do something. I finally came to my senses and aimed that high-powered Crossman pellet rifle. In an instant, I managed to fire a single shot at the mongrel fowl and then ran as fast as my legs would carry me. I bet that thing had a ten-foot wingspread; it had a long beak and claws. I really couldn't see any claws, but that's how they looked when I saw 'em on T.V. (It could have probably carried me away if I hadn't been brave enough to shoot at it.) I knew right then when I saw that bird Earnest and Mammy's house was haunted; there was no doubt anymore. It wouldn't stop me, though; I was tough. Some giant pre-historic vulture wouldn't keep me away. I knew there was strength in numbers, so when I went back to the house I always took somebody with me. It had nothing to do with me being scared or anything either.

Like I said earlier, we knew intruders had come on to the property around the old house. They had already made new paths straight to the house. Well, maybe they weren't exactly intruders, but they were not boys from the grove. The Connell brothers, Rusty Welch, and Mike Parsons were a few who visited. We all rode the school bus together and some of them even went to High Point Church, so they weren't exactly strangers. To be honest with you, I got to be pretty good friends with some of those boys.

Mike Parsons and I started to spend some time together. We were the same age, went to the same church and school, and had even been in Scouts together. He lived about five or six houses below the Pecan Grove. Mike had a twin sister, Andrea, but they didn't look anything alike, thank goodness. Well, what I mean by that is, I didn't like pretty boys then, and I don't like pretty boys now. Andrea looked very much like her mom and that was good, but Mike was the spittin' image of his daddy. Unlike me, he was a pretty intelligent and fairly sharp guy; he had sandy brown hair, dark eyes, and a brave streak in him, just like me. I told you it was good that his sister looked like his mama. The reason I say that is because she was prettier than any speckled puppy I had ever seen. I always kinda liked her, but I never let on, because that was Mike's sister.

Mr. Parsons worked for the Georgia Forestry Commission as the head forest ranger. Mrs. Helen, Mike's mom, kept the books at People's Drugstore on the square. That has absolutely nothing to do with the story. I just figured some of the more nosy people would want to know.

Well, anyway, Mike and I were talking and trying to figure out what we would do after school one day. We decided to walk to Earnest's and Mammy's from my house. That little old red-clay road had about washed out. Nobody really kept it up, but it was still a good path for walking or riding bikes. We had made some pretty good bike ramps down through there. You never knew what you may run up on, maybe a rabbit or a squirrel, a covey of quail may fly up in front of us. That 'bout scared the crap out of me every time it happened, too. You have no idea if you ain't never had a covey of quail fly right up in front of you. Anyhow, we got to the back of the house and stepped through the back door. We looked around a minute or two. There really wasn't a lot to look at; it was just two bare, unpainted rooms. The holes in the sheetrock and busted out windows didn't help anything either. We walked right on through to the front porch. You could hear the tin flap when the wind was up. The old rusty roof had worked loose and made a horrid sound. The old floor was rough sawmill lumber and the steps leading out front were made of about the same stuff. The porch was held up by old field rock that had been carefully laid. Somebody had cut some cedar logs and that's what the old porch post was made out of. There was really no yard much, just red clay. There were a few wild roses growing just past the red-clay yard around some huge oak trees.

Mike and I sat down on the front steps and started a conversation. I can't remember what we were talking about, but I can tell you it had to be important. Usually, anytime I went for the woods, my little feist dog, Sally, would follow me. I hadn't seen her for a little while, though. She probably had a squirrel treed somewhere. This was in the middle of the day and nobody else was around. Mike or I, either one of us are not boys that would exaggerate stories or hear things that were not there either. Right in the middle of our conversation, I looked at Mike and Mike looked at me. I said to him, "Did you hear that?"

He said, "Sounds like footsteps."

I said, "Yeah..." We both peeked back in the house and the noise stopped. We tried our best to act like there was nothing to it. There was, though, because within seconds, we heard the noise again. This time, it sounded like it was getting closer. We took no time to investigate this time. We ran like two shot dogs. As I looked back, I know I saw a ghost coming out of a window on the side of the house. I don't know if it was Earnest or Mammy but we must have interrupted something. You always heard the expression, 'You look like you seen a ghost.' I'm here to tell you, that afternoon, Ricky Darby and Mike Parsons done seen something they won't never forget.

We got back to the house and started talking about what had just happened. I went right in my house and got the pellet rifle. I would have got the shotgun, but I knew my daddy would have had my hide. Now I ain't gonna lie to you, that scared ten years off my life. We decided we had to investigate further, though. Best way to do that was get reinforcements. Brent Mask came up in just the nick of time. We told him what had happened. He went home and got his BB gun and went straight back to the scene of the crime. By this time, probably an hour had passed. The tactical squad was ready to put an end to any ghost or haint in or around the Pecan Grove. As you can figure, we would never go right up to the house. I mean, the police always had a perimeter; things would be no different for us.

When we got close enough to where we could see the window where that ghost was comin' out after us, then we would be close enough. Remember, our safety was of utmost importance. The three of us eased back down the old road that we had run out of an hour or so earlier. We got just past a little clearing in the woods and tried to find our best vantage point. As we all could see the outline of the house, we started looking for the window. The side window where we had seen this thing was open. A couple of the glass panes had been shot out of it, too. Sure enough, when we all got to where we could see it, the ghost was still there. We whispered, "We gotta shoot that thing," not thinking if it was a ghost it was already dead. Our bullets would go clean through it, but it seemed to be the right thing to do at the time. I had my pellet rifle pumped up ten times and I fired the first round. Brent fired his BB gun at will. Glass was shattering, we were screaming but the object never moved. You could see through it and it was almost a light blue color. I had never seen a ghost up to this point so I had no idea what they should look like. When we ceased fire and felt as though we had done everything possible, we headed home dumbfounded. We had no intention of trying to assess the situation anymore than we already had.

For several weeks, we didn't make an attempt to even get close to that old haunted house. We had heard other boys (outsiders) were hanging out around the old house and hadn't seen anything. Finally, our curiosity got the best of us so we bravely made our trek back to the spooky dwelling. We walked in the back door with a lot of apprehension. To be honest with you, we were ready to run if we saw anything that even resembled a haint. This time, the first thing I saw was a light blue, sheer curtain, torn, and weather-beaten, flapping out the window where I thought I had seen the ghost. Upon further investigation, we saw pellets and BBs buried in the unpainted sheetrock. Could it have all been just our wild imaginations? Nobody will ever know, now will they? What I believe is that was just coincidental, because we know what we saw. There is one thing for certain, though: I AIN'T afraid of no ghost.

AT THE PRISON HOSPITAL

The sergeant got up and said to me, "I know why Hartley wanted you now, gets your mind off all the junk we have to deal with around here." He stuck out his hand and grasped mine tightly looking me straight in the eyes. "It's been a real pleasure, sir, and I appreciate you being here; it means a lot to this old fart."

Jake looked at the burly guard and spouted, "Ain't you got something to do?"

Johnny got a boyish grin on his face and asked, "Been skinny-dippin' lately?"

I said to the brothers, "You might guess what you are gonna hear about next."

CHAPTER 7

Skinny-dippin' and High-steppin'

Every red-blooded American boy has dreams and fantasies. The Boyz in the Grove were no different. I had seen *Gilligan's Island* one too many times and I just wanted to be stranded on an Island one day with a beauty like Ginger on it. It would have been nice to have had a genie that would grant your every desire. It was obvious we would not see any of those things, so we had to make do. I guess my daddy didn't believe in vacations. There were times I could have imagined lying out on the beach and watching bikini babes. The best of that I ever saw was when my sister would let me spend the night with her and her husband, David. We would get up early and go to Pine Island. Callaway Gardens was there and had a pretty nice beach, but it was not the ocean. We could ride the paddleboats or swim. There was even a circus show. She had a girl from across the street go with us to keep me company. Linda looked out for her little brother in a pretty major way.

Other than that, the boys were always looking for a place to get cool in the summer time. We did have a water hose but our folks would tell us after a few minutes, "Turn off that water, you are gonna run the well dry." We were boys of adventure and there was uncharted territory to be discovered. We started at the creek in front of Earnest and

Mammy's old place. We would run through the creek or maybe try and dam up a place. There were big snappin' turtles and crawdads around that creek and it was not a place we could swim, although we did manage to get wet.

Each summer, we got a little braver and adventured out a little farther. The river was about a half mile from the house. There was a good-sized creek that fed in to it and we loved playin' in that water but it was not deep enough to swim in and the river was too deep. I guess you see we had not yet found a swimmin' hole that fit our boyish needs.

I had been introduced to the railroad tracks that crossed East End Road by my daddy. There were some pretty cool places off the tracks. I got to see and cross my first railroad trestle and found where some old military equipment was stored. I even saw my first deer when we were walkin' down the tracks. What Daddy didn't know was that he showed me and the boys our first real swimmin' hole. Well, he didn't ever let on like he knew anyway. This was a little pond right off the tracks. You would have to watch for briars and climb over the barbed wire fence, but there it sat pretty as you please.

Johnny (Jacob's little brother, remember him, the smoker?) and I went to this place more than anybody else. After seeing how long it took cutoffs to dry, we figured we would swim in our underwear, but it left a muddy stain on them and you could never make up a big enough tale for your folks to believe. So, with our finite wisdom, we thought we would just leave our clothes on the bank and go skinny-dippin'. The little fish were kind of pesky but we got used to that. They would nibble in places your mama was not allowed to touch. We had a ball, and I reckon with all the fun we were having, we didn't realize we were getting a little loud. I didn't mention we were trespassing, did I?

As I am sure you can imagine, boys really don't realize just how much their screams travel. You got it, the owner of the property heard us. You would think he would just come to the pond and explain to us the dangers of swimming without adult supervision. But no, he wanted to scare the living daylights out of us. The first thing we heard was "HEYYY.....YOU BUNCH OF DELINQUENTS, WHAT THE HELL DO YOU THINK YOU ARE DOIN', I'M A GOOD MINE TO KILL YOU BOTH," then a shotgun blast; I was too young to die. Let me tell you, all you could see was butts and elbows. We managed to get our clothes and get lost. With briars, bushes, and barbed wire fence, we didn't get a single scratch. I did however taste my heart when it ran up into my throat. You would think after an episode like that, it would teach us a lesson, but that just made us a lot sneakier.

We would skinny-dip many other times in that old pond but we were just much quieter and didn't linger very long. There was one more time that is really worth mentioning, though. It was the day the train stopped in Dixie. Sounds like a good name for a country song, don't it?

Before we cooled off that day, we thought we would see how a train could tear up pine trees. Loggers had been in the area and cut many of the pines for lumber. I don't know if you've ever come in after loggers, but they leave a mess. The mess quickly became an opportunity to a couple of rambunctious boys. We started gathering saplings and limbs and piled them across the tracks. We figured when the train come by, it would make a heck of a mess. The train usually ran about 3:00, so we hid down in the thicket to see what would happen. Let me just say, our plans got thwarted. The train was goin' real slow when it came into the straightaway where all the brush was piled. It looked like it might stop. It did, and Johnny and I were scared to death. Two men got off the train and started moving the brush. You might have guessed it. They spotted us and started after us. I'm gonna tell ya I ran like a bat out of hell. Never knew I could run so fast, but I ran slap back to the house. I was wearin' a pair of cutoffs. My T-shirt was in my back pocket and I was barefooted. Any other time, I would have been cut by briars and my feet would have been eaten up. This time, though, I didn't have a scratch anywhere.

After that incident, swimming in my birthday suit didn't interest me nearly as much. At least not until such a time someone of the opposite sex might want to reciprocate. Us boys had already seen girls naked in some girly magazines we had confiscated. I had never seen any girl naked in person up until that point. I was mesmerized by the thought.

A lot of years have passed since then, but there is one thing I know for sure: Ain't no man gonna keep me from doing what I want to do if I am determined enough.

That determination helped me a number of years later. A new friend, Mac, who was several years older, and I were about to experience another naked truth. My mama thought Mac might be queer, to enjoy the company of someone my age. We hooked up originally because I had a four-man raft and floated the Alcovy River. Believe you me, that boy was straighter than an arrow and had some sexy female friends.

We were out riding one sultry summer night when we ran up on three of the most vulumpcious beauties. These teenage girls seemed like they might have been around, if you follow me. Anyway, we all piled in a car together. We headed down Highway 278 out of town. While talking, we made a unanimous decision. We would scale the fence at the Elks Club pool and go skinny-dippin'. When we got there, Mac and I helped the girls over and then they discovered an open gate. Long story short, we all got in the water with our underwear and stripped down to the skinny skin skin. It was about to really heat up when we saw headlights. You guessed it, the sheriff's deputy drove up and saw us. The deputy asked if we had permission to be there at about the same time he noticed a pile of clothes next to the pool. He never even got out of the car, but we did know our fate was in his hands. We all believed it anyway. Another strike out, he told us to get our clothes on and leave. I did get wet, but that was about as far as I got, that night anyway....

IN THE HOSPITAL ROOM

Johnny was about to leave and head back to Oxford, where he lived at the time. He looked at Jake and asked, "Do you remember when Darby got his COOL glasses?"

Jake was not even a little kind when he looked at me and said, "You mean old four eyes?"

I happened to call 'em "spec-tickles" and I never claimed they were cool, I told 'em both. "Now that was a while back," I said to 'em....

CHAPTER 8

"Spec-tickles" Ain't Cool

There are a few things that are just downright embarrassing to a young, impressionable boy. I mean things like your mama seeing you naked or walking in on your mama and daddy while they are romancing...Not that either one ever happened now. Maybe standing in front of a crowd not knowing your zipper's down could be one, too. You get the picture. I just couldn't imagine going through the humiliation of wearing one of those retainers that alert every medal detector in three states. That's right, we didn't even have metal detectors like that at the time. The other thing was having to wear glasses. A cool kid should not have to wear glasses in the 60s. I mean there was only one style back then: UGLY. All your friends started calling you names like "four eyes" and "dork." At eleven or twelve years old, you got a reputation to uphold. After all, you will soon be a teenager. I put it off as long as I could but the adults in my life were getting wise to me and my foolproof schemes. What I know now is any village idiot could see I was blind as a bat.

I started off by sitting close to the blackboard so I could make out what the teacher was writing. I pretended like I wanted to be studious but I really just wanted to see. I would ask the teacher questions so maybe she wouldn't call on me.

The problem was when we had assigned seats, I squinted so bad some people thought I might be half Oriental or something.

Somebody always has to ruin a perfectly good plan and let the cat out of the bag, though. In this case, it was my fourth-grade teacher, Mrs. Richardson. Her husband was the school superintendent. She called Mama and Daddy in for a conference because she had concerns about my grades. I still can't understand, a C was supposed to be average and a D was still passing. But no, Ms. Goody-Two-Shoes thought I ought to be making As and Bs. When this teacher and my parents got together, they came up with their own schemes. My teacher said to Mama and Daddy, "Ricky is a delightful student. I just believe he needs glasses."

You could have knocked me over with a feather. They knew a lot more about me than they had let on. It must have been a conspiracy or something, because my mama immediately agreed that she would do whatever necessary to help me improve my grades. She made such a scholarly decision. I expect you would probably say, oh that's so sweet. Obviously you didn't grow up when or where I did. If you were to help your child today, it would be far different than then. It could mean a new computer program or special tutoring and even if a kid needed their eyes examined now, that ain't such a bad thing. It was like holding up a sign and saying, "I JUST BECAME A GEEK" with me. My mama said, "First thing you are going do is get your eyes checked. Your daddy is going to take you to the eye doctor and get you some glasses." She told me after I got my glasses, I would stay in my room until I could show her my grades were getting better. I thought to myself that could mean years. I would probably be given bread and water and one visitor each week like any other prisoner.

Well, when Daddy and I got to the doctor's office, I was scared spitless. Everyone knew Dr. William Dodd in downtown Covington; he had been ruining kids' lives with glasses for years. Not only was he downtown but he was also throwing distance from the courthouse. Guess whose office was the first you came to? Sheriff James Otter, yep, in case I ran, the doctor had the sheriff on his side, too. This conspiracy theory was making more and more sense. Dr. Geekmaker had it all figured out. His office was narrow and long; there were several real dark rooms in the back. When he came up to get me, I had no idea what may happen next. Dr. Dodd looked at me and said, "Ricky, you can come with me now." I sat down in this weird-looking chair, and he told me to read the letters on the back wall. I knew right then he was in on all this, too. I mean he must have talked to mama and the teacher because all I could see was a blur. After that, it was utter confusion. He pulled this contraption in front of my face and told me to lean up and look into it. One eye was covered and then he would say, "Can you see clearer with this one or this one." Then he would say, "Is this better or this? Ok, what about this?" This must have gone on for hours. I quickly felt like I must have been in some sort of concentration camp for twelve-year-olds. It was definitely beginning to work. I thought to myself, *Just get me out of this place and I will make honor roll.*

The torture had only just begun. When the doctor finally let me up from the chair, we walked back to the front of the office together. He was the bearer of bad news. "Looks like you do need glasses, but the good news is you get to pick out the frames." That wouldn't be very hard since there were only two styles: girls and boys, and two colors: gray or black. Times have changed, haven't they?

A week later, I picked up my glasses. The doc had to fit me and be sure I could see out of them. What would I do now? The girls wouldn't give me the time of day, not that they had before, but still…I figured my friends would be real scarce. Who wants to hang out with four eyes anyway? I mean this was devastating, a life scar. I looked weird and I knew it. To this day, very few people see my school pictures during those years. It just brings back such horrid memories.

There was one thing I learned, though: my friends really didn't care if I wore glasses or not. They didn't even care about what others said. We were friends. That is really something because I found that today, there are those who claim to be your friend until you hit a bump in the road. Then there are those who are with you through thick and thin. Glasses or not, bumps or not, we all need a few friends that don't care if you are popular. They don't even care if you are right, they are just friends….

BACK TO JAKE'S ROOM

Old Jake's tired eyes stared into mine. He looked at me and said, "I feel like I wasted a lot of my life, Rick. I wish I could go back and do some things over, but I can't. It would have been nice if my grandchildren could talk about spending Sunday afternoon at my house. I have old memories like that. I know you do, too. It would be nice if I could walk 'em through High Point cemetery and share about some of those saints who were laid to rest there. I sure wish I could have smelled that musty old church again. You know it won't be long till I get to the other side, though."

I grabbed Jake's frail old hand and told him, "Sit back, old friend, I want you to recollect, not fret. There are some old precious memories that we all hold dear."

Jake looked up at me and said, "Oh yeah, you did look like a geek."

CHAPTER 9

Precious Memories
How They Linger

I guess one of my favorite places to go while I was growin' up was to Granny and Paw Paw's on Sunday afternoon. About once every couple of months, the whole family would meet after church. I liked to get there a little early because the driveway would fill up fast. Sometimes, we would park next door at the Haralsons. They loved Granny and Paw Paw 'bout as much as we did. All my cousins would be there and we would really enjoy being together. Their families came from miles around.

Granny and Paw Paw lived at the corner of Newton Drive and Conyers Street. The house was right small but somehow we all got in. Granny's kitchen was the biggest room in the house and it had two tables in it. That was where some ate, but it also became our buffet line. I can smell her fried chicken as it comes off the stove and see those cat-head biscuits steamin' as they came out of the oven. Mama must have learned to cook from Granny because she flat knew what she was doing. You would always see homemade pickles and relish, fresh tomatoes, and spring onions to go with the vegetables. She would have fresh speckled butterbeans, field peas, and the greens of the season. I would try to sneak through and get me a piece of fried fatback before we ate.

I'm gonna tell you about her famous chocolate cake in a few minutes. It would have won first place at the county fair, but it would have never made it out of the house.

Granny was the sweetest woman I had ever met. She was short and round. She was just plump enough, though, because her hugs were like cuddling up to a soft pillow. It seemed like she was always wearing an apron and a smile. Granny was a Godly woman; she would always see that we prayed and she would talk about the Lord on a regular basis. She was never ashamed to share her faith either. She would tell us, "You can't be ashamed of Jesus." I guess she kept our family together better than most anybody these days. After all, that kind of love is contagious.

Paw Paw was Granny's third husband. Her first one abandoned her and her second one died. Loy Skelton was Paw Paw's name and I thought he was a fine man. He always treated us well and loved my Granny. It hadn't always been that way, though. When Granny and Paw Paw met, he was a rounder. He loved his liquor and was foul-mouthed. Somehow, my Granny loved him right on into the Kingdom of God. He took her to church with him every time the door was open. He ended up with twenty-five years of perfect attendance in Sunday school at Calvary Baptist Church. Calvary had been at Covington Mill for a long time and that was the church they called home.

Let me get back to the Sunday dinner. When all of us came in and Uncle Johnny (the Baptist preacher) asked the blessing, we would grab our plates and start filling. We would eat in every room in the house except the bathroom and the living room. The living room was off limits because it was just used for special occasions and some of us may break Granny's knick-knacks. The hardwood floors in that room shined like a basketball court. It was a room for grown-ups only. There was a side porch and a front porch we would go to as well. There was usually a good twenty-five or so there. After we finished the main meal, we would get dessert. Besides chocolate cake, we would have pecan, lemon, sweet potato, or coconut pie. My favorite, along with my Uncle Samuel, was chocolate cake. He would always kid me about who could eat the most. It didn't look like it bothered either of us because we were both skinny. I was named after him (Samuel Richard) and I loved Uncle Samuel. I remember when he bought a 1965 Mustang. It was a fine vehicle and he was the only uncle with a sports car. All my aunts and uncles were neat but there was something about Samuel. It might have been because he spent time with us and just let us act like kids. Sometimes, he even acted that way himself.

With aunts and uncles come cousins, and I mean lots of them. Uncle Samuel and his wife Eleanor only had one boy, Sammy. He married way over his head; she was a real pretty woman. My Aunt Helen had three girls and a boy, Doug. Her husband had died but she seemed to do pretty well on her own. Then there was Uncle Johnny and Faye, they had all girls except for Mel, their only son. Then Uncle J.C. and Frankie had three boys and a girl, I believe. Mama had stepsisters and I ain't even gonna attempt to name them all. Anyway, they were all ages and a good number of them somewhere around my age. We didn't sit around and play board games or watch television; we got outside and found something to do. We could take a long walk, play in the woods behind the garden, ramble in the garage, or climb a pecan tree. There were a couple of new things we discovered. One was playing hubcap and several other silly games like "one, two, three red light." Another thing we did was something that still turns my mouth inside out when I think about it. We ate pomegranates off Granny's bush. She had a huge bush just as you came in the driveway. We would dare each other to take the first bite. That first bite would make you pucker up so that you could kiss a mule right in the mouth and never even taste it. In case you have never

51

tasted a pomegranate, they had little pods that you bite into and spit out the seeds; sour can't describe it.

Memories were molded during those years, things that will never be forgotten. There were triumphs and tragedies, victories and defeats. I get right emotional thinking it has been over thirty years since we all met at Granny's for Sunday dinner. I wonder will my children and grandchildren have any such memories of their childhood at my house? I can only hope, but I can't imagine the food tasting as good.

You know what, while I'm sharing memories, you just got to hear about the old country church I grew up in....

When you grow up in the center of the Bible Belt, going to church is quite important. My daddy saw to it I was there every time the door was open. He may have not always been there but he saw to it that I was. High Point Baptist Church was only about four miles down the road from the house. My family had been a part of that church for long time. My daddy had laid both his parents to rest right there in that cemetery. Little did I know at the time, I would be doing the same thing, many years later.

When I was growin' up, there was an old clapboard building we all called our church sanctuary. Next to it was a block educational building where all the Sunday school rooms were. The preacher and his family lived in a brick house right behind the church. They didn't have a lot of privacy but he could walk to work.

The first preacher I remember was Preacher Hudson Moody. I remember sometimes he preached like he was mad or something because his face would get beet red. He had a slew of children and one of his girls was actually the same age as me. He left the church when I was probably eleven years old. He preached at another church across town, but he never forgot our family.

I remember we always played around the church while the grownups talked after the service. Right behind the church was a little wooded area where an old Model T body sat, rusting away. There we pretended it was our car, a spaceship, or a fort. We played hide and seek, kick ball, and chase. Anyway, there are a lot of kids that have vivid memories of their childhood at High Point. I wonder how Dennis Rainey, Clay Henderson, Keith Connell, or Ivy Carter would describe our days together.

There were several people in that little country church who made a difference in many lives. Most of them didn't even know what they were doing. Well, I didn't either, but I do now. What was going on was they were giving something money can't buy. Things like love, patience, gentleness, goodness, and understanding. That kind of stuff is priceless. Anyway, they must have made an impact because there is a soft spot in my heart for a lot of those people, several of whom are walkin' streets of gold right now.

I want to try and paint a picture right now. This is good stuff and you got to see it. The old church sat about a hundred feet off the road with a gravel parking lot right in front of it. To the left of the church was the cemetery with granite markers scattered all around. You could see fresh cut flowers on some of the graves. Over to the right corner was a sign made of white-painted wood and metal that had slide-in black steel letters. There were three gray concrete steps that went all the way across the front of the entry where you came in. There had been a porch at one time on the front but it had been closed in to make a vestibule. It was six or eight feet deep and had two varnished doors that could be opened to go right into the sanctuary.

Most everybody has been in one of these old churches before. It has a distinct smell. I don't know how to describe it, the smell that causes memories to flood. I guess if I could go in there today and just take a deep breath, it would make me a little teary-eyed. I guess it was the combination of old wood, plaster board, and hardwood floors. You probably say none of that has a smell. Obviously, you didn't grow up like I did. In the center of the front of the church, there on the Communion table, every Sunday, were fresh cut flowers. They were always in memory of somebody, or to remember an anniversary. We always knew who was being honored, because it was in the church bulletin.

None of the pews were padded; they were solid wood, black and white ends with varnished seats. Some of the women brought their own cushions. Then, on the platform were two big, tall, padded kings' chairs. They kind of looked like a throne to me. These were gold velvet with wide armrests and thick padding. Usually, the preacher and choir director sat in them. On each side on the front wall was a big wood board that had slide-in numbers. One was for Sunday school attendance and the other one was for the Training Union. They were important because they told how many brought their Bible, how much offering, and all sorts of other important statistical data. The pulpit was big and matched the rest of the furniture. I can still see those tall, narrow windows with regular glass; we weren't uptown enough to have stained glass. From time to time, those old windows had to be raised to let the fresh air in. If we filled the church, they had to bring out the chairs. These were not metal folding chairs, but oak with cane bottoms. Maybe you get the general idea.

Between Sunday school and church, some of the men would come out to the side of the church and smoke before greeting everybody. I won't ever forget men like Mr. Thomas Johnson and Mr. Otis Hayes whom I saw every Sunday having a smoke. Then standing at the door to the sanctuary were two ladies giving out bulletins and greeting the people. The bulletins were typed and copied, but sometimes with typos. In the summer, we used funeral home fans to cool off because there was no air conditioning back then.

I can still see Mr. James leading the choir and singing his heart out. He was a robust man with a big voice. Some of those old songs, I like to sing now like "Victory in Jesus," "Onward Christian Soldiers," "When We all get to Heaven," "I'll Fly Away," and of course, "Precious Memories." One of those old songs, however, played a serious role in my life: "Just as I Am."

During a Youth Revival one night, when I was around thirteen years old, something happened. The visiting preacher had preached a strong sermon and all of it made sense. Hell is hot, but Heaven is sweet. Back then, preachers talked about hell like it was a place we ought to shun and heaven a place we ought to go when we leave this world. There was a time or two I got a little scared. Well, that night, after the second verse of "Just As I Am," my knuckles were white from holding on the back of that pew. We should have been singing "I Shall Not Be Moved." I can't even tell you exactly how it happened, all I know was I found myself at the altar of that little Baptist church. I was standing there just a-crying. Finally, the preacher came over and asked me, "What can the Lord do for you tonight, son?"

I told him I wanted to get saved. I prayed with him that night and the Lord touched my soul and Jesus became my Savior. When I walked back to my pew, I felt cleaner than ever before. God must have used some of that Mr. Clean on me. Ain't nothing like my Jesus; he put my feet on the solid rock.

I wanted to do something, but I had no idea what. This was when bus ministry was really getting off the ground, churches all around had buses. We had bought two old school buses from the Board of Education. One of the men in the church ran a body shop and had agreed to paint them. They ended up mint green and white. You could see 'em comin' a mile away. Anyway, I was able to help with that ministry every week, visiting and riding on the bus, to take kids and others who didn't have their own transportation.

We were not like a lot of the churches where everybody was Brother So-and-So or Sister So-and-So. With us, it was either Mr. or Ms. They had to be real old if we called 'em by their last name. We had men like Mr. Ed (not the talking horse either) or Mr. Otis; there was Mr. Leon and Mr. Jimmy. Really, all the ladies were not even Ms. but all Miss, no matter whether they were married or not. Ladies like Miss Nora, Miss Mary Frances, Miss Dot, and Miss Jean and so on and so on.

There was something about some of these people, though. They didn't try and impress anybody; they did make an impact on me, though. I have got to tell you about Mr. Leon first. He was the boys' Sunday school teacher about the same time I got saved. I hate to tell you this, but he wasn't all that exciting. Sometimes, he had us read the Sunday school lesson and would then ask us questions. He even made us pray aloud. I guess we would call that interaction today. There was one Sunday, however, I don't guess I will ever forget. It was right before Christmas and Mr. Leon asked us a real thought-provoking question. He said, "Boys, what do you want Jesus to give you for Christmas?" Some of us came up with some real dumb answers and they were self-serving, too. There was one boy in our class who got to us all that day. Mr. Leon said, "Keith, what do you want Jesus to give you?"

He looked at us all with tears in his eyes and said, "I want Jesus to not let my daddy get drunk this Christmas." You know what? We all found out Jesus did just that for our friend.

Several years passed and a new church was built across the road. Bryant Steele oversaw the construction. That building was filled with memories, too. I remember Preacher Mobley and his family came after they left the mission field.

They had lived in Japan for over five years. That man really knew God. There are just too many things to share.

There is one thing for sure, I was proud to call High Point Baptist Church my church. I had no problem telling people where I went to church and where I was going one day, once I left this world.

BACK IN JAKE'S ROOM

As I finished my story, a young, attractive nurse with a real soft Southern accent came in the room. She said, "Mr. Hartley, sweetie, I got to get your blood pressure and take your temperature."

Jake looked at her and commented, "Honey, you go do anything you want to with me. You want me to have Mr. Darby leave?"

"So this is Mr. Darby; Jacob Hartley, you were supposed to tell us when he got here. I've got eight nurses who are waiting to hear one of his stories. Now, we are gonna steal him for just one story, besides you need to rest."

I told Jacob I had to see these nurses and I would be back shortly. As I followed the young nurse, she turned and extended her hand. "Mr. Darby, my name is Penny and we have all heard about your storytelling. You don't mind spending a few minutes with us, do you?" We rounded the corner toward a small conference room. I told Penny I would be honored to share a story. We walked into the room and I smelled the bold aroma of fresh brewed coffee. There were nurses all around the conference table. Penny showed me to my seat at the head of the table and asked me if she could fix me some fresh java. Of course, I gladly accepted. Cream and sugar, please.

A fairly well-proportioned nurse looked at me and said, "We hear you were quite a romantic when you were a young buck." She introduced herself as Jane and asked if I remembered her. My heart skipped a beat as I told her she didn't look familiar. But there was a Jane I knew a long time ago. The flirty nurse grinned and said, "And just how well did you know this girl?"

My response to her was, "Well, I guess you will just have to hear the story......."

CHAPTER 10

New Neighbors and
Fresh Romance

The old saying "Boys will be boys" couldn't be truer about us boys in the Pecan Grove. I mean, we loved mischief, adventure, and those of the opposite sex. Brent Mask was probably my very best friend. We spent a lot of time together as you might expect. Brent and I had even set the woods a fire one time. At this particular time, we were more interested in being good neighbors.

We heard about this family that had moved in the old house back of the Pecan Grove. It was the same house my brother Larry's friend, Idous Lawson, had lived in several years earlier. They had rented it from the Cook family who owned all the land behind us. There were several kids there around our age. Brent was a year younger than me and so some of these in that family were even a few years younger. I can't recall all the names but I remember Joe, the oldest son, and Jane, the oldest daughter.

We all got to be good friends real fast. Joe was like one of us as far as Brent and I were concerned. We rode bikes and built some forts. That is not what sticks out in my mind the most, though. Joe's daddy enjoyed cold beer on a fairly regular basis. As a matter of fact, he enjoyed it enough that Joe could sneak one out of the house every once in a while.

Joe was a quiet boy but we convinced him to do whatever we asked him. Here I am, ain't been saved long wanting to indulge in the evils of alcohol consumption. I really just wanted to see what it tasted like. I had heard some say it was delicious and others say it tasted like horse pee. I had no intention of becoming a sippin' saint like some folks that went to one of those big churches uptown.

Here we are Brent, Joe, and me, hid in the woods close to Joe's house, about to experiment with our first malt beverage. It was a Carlings Black Label, in a twelve-ounce can. We moved back a little further in the woods so nobody would see us. Joe popped the top and it spewed a little. We then all bravely took a sip. I knew it was supposed to taste good but for the life of me, I couldn't make myself enjoy it. Joe went back to the well several more times over the next few months and as far as we know his daddy never suspected a thing. To be honest, though, it was not Joe I was most interested in; it was his sister, Jane.

Jane had brown curly hair and pretty eyes, but she also had something most girls her age didn't have: boobs. She was well endowed and I was hooked. It didn't take long before I was able to squeeze her heart until we became an item. The boys didn't like it but my testosterone did. Jane and I walked around holding hands and acting right silly to most who saw us. I had those goo-goo eyes and a racing heart. What the other boys didn't know wouldn't hurt 'em. This young boy had a plan; I mean it was not every day you got a chance to have a girl like Jane. As we talked, I convinced her we had to find a place to make out. To be honest, it was a first for me and her both. It was a little scary thinking about this but we agreed on a spot. Since her mama wouldn't let her leave the yard with me, we thought we could get together on the far side of the house. There was just one window there and we could hear if anybody was coming. Jane even got us an old quilt to stretch out on.

I told Brent he would have to keep Joe busy because I had some real business to tend to. He agreed but he had eyes for Joe's other sister. I don't recollect her name, but I was not enamored with her either. Brent tried to do his part, but it was tough with all the kids and animals around. It's hard to do serious loving when a dog wants to lick you in the face. As hard as I tried, it seemed to always be a no-hitter if you get my drift. I never had kissed anybody except my mama, my sisters, well maybe my granny and some of my aunts, oh yeah I had kissed my dog. Don't you tell anybody I was kissing up on my dog either. Rumors get started that way. I loved my animals and sometimes, I would kiss 'em on top of the head. I hadn't kissed any dog or anybody else right in the mouth either. Somebody said something about using your tongue, too. Finally Jane and I just decided distractions or not, we were gonna do some huggin' and kissin'. I kissed her on the cheek first because I was familiar with that. Then I looked her in the eyes and tried lookin' down her blouse but couldn't see anything. Our lips connected, and we smacked one right on out. It was not romantic in the least.

We kept on practicing, though; I even tried using my tongue one time but I thought we would both choke. I always had visions of those sugar plums, though, at least that's what I called 'em. Those two beautiful vulumpcious, well, how do I say it, breasts, there I got it out. It really was not that hard either. There are parts of the human anatomy we boys are just enamored with. Mine just happened to be 36D. Jane never let on like she knew I was so awestruck by her and of course that BODY. I think she might have been lookin' for love in all the wrong places. At any rate, she burned a spot in my heart. Well, it may have been lower than my heart. It has been a long time but visions of sugar plums still have a special meaning.

Even though that family lived in our neighborhood only a short time, I was able to experience some real interesting things. There are several things that might still be worth remembering, too:

1. Greeting new neighbors can be a rewarding experience.

2. Learning to kiss somebody besides your mama 'n 'em or your dog requires steady concentration.

3. Sex education in the sixties was a whole lot better firsthand than watching some slideshow and one of your teachers tell you about it.

4. Your tongue ought to be used for talking not kissin'.

5. Be sure to get a dependable look-out before you start romancing.

6. Girls always smell better than boys. (Just information you ought to know.)

7. X-ray glasses don't see through clothes, I don't care if you paid $2.00 for a pair.

I had not even become a teenager yet and had already had some serious experiences that some boys my age would never imagine. Who would know what the years to come would hold? The teenage years were gaining on me fast and I was ready to see what sewing wild oats really meant....

ABOUT THEN

The nurses all grinned and giggled and said, "Her name is not Jane either; it's Vicki. We just wanted to see your reaction." All the nurses thanked me for sharing my story and welcomed me back any time.

I excused myself and headed back to Jake's room. I didn't want to wake him, but I knew I had to get back to

Commerce and he needed his rest. Jake was almost asleep.
I said, "Jake, you need your rest, buddy, and I need to head
back. I want you to know something, though. I'll be praying
for you."

THE DEPARTURE

As I wished Jacob the best and started to leave the room,
he said, "One more thing, Darby, don't ever stop telling those
stories."

I said to him that would never happen. His next statement
really surprised me. He asked would I record everything I
could remember about our teen years? "Write all the details
you can think about even past April of '71."

I promised I would try even though it had been over
thirty-five years.

The minute he said that, it seemed as though I had been
given permission; I could relive those teen years again. It
may just have been the revelation I needed to put some sort
of closure on that part of my life. I had talked a little about
things that happened, but over thirty years later, I could
walk through it again. The more I thought, the stronger the
feelings got. Not everybody has the opportunity to relive
their teenage years.

Hartley was right, it must be recorded—the good, the
bad, and the ugly. There were many wild and crazy stories
that were yet to be told and now the excuse I had used for
years was no longer valid. As thoughts raced through my
mind, I could almost smell the old rum-flavored cigars and
feel the kick of my old sixteen-gauge double-barrel shotgun.
I could vividly remember the pain of a broken heart after
my true love had told me it just was not gonna work out. I
felt the confusion and fear of ninth grade at Newton High. I
could sense my heart racing when I rode in Jacob's '64 Ford
at over one hundred miles an hour.

I thought, when this is written on paper, it cannot just be my ideas and stories. Somehow, when my grown children and their cousins and the children of every person mentioned looks at the words they are able to step into these stories and feel what we felt. I hurried to my car so I could just get my composure. That was not going to happen, though. Before I could get my key in the door to unlock it, I laughed out loud when I thought about my long lanky legs and my pants up past my belly button. I thought about swallowing tobacco juice because someone wouldn't let me spit. Then my mind quickly raced to an April afternoon, the hair on the back of my neck stood straight up and I felt a tingling up my spine and looked at the hair on my arms standing at attention, too. I wished I could just leave all that pain alone, but that was where I had to use the wisdom of a half-century old man and faded thoughts and dreams.....

I reached into the console of my truck and pulled out a Carpenters CD. It was part one of those oldies packages I had bought in a set a couple of years ago. When I pulled out and opened the case to make my one-and-a-half-hour ride home, the strangest thing happened—It was the song...That was the last confirmation I needed to heed Hartley's request. It was my hope that somehow he would be able to give the final approval when I had finished what would prove to be a painstaking adventure into the past. The song "Yesterday Once More" was what I listened intently to when I hit the road and headed back toward my home in Commerce. Here are the words to that song.

> *When I was young I'd listen to the radio*
> *Waitin' for my favorite songs*
> *When they played I'd sing along*
> *It made me smile.*
>
> *Those were such happy times*
> *And not so long ago*

How I wondered where they'd gone
But they're back again
Just like a long lost friend
All the songs I'd loved so well

When they get to the part
Where he's breakin' her heart
It can really make me cry
Just like before
It's yesterday once more

Lookin' back on how it was
In years gone by
And good times that I had
Makes today seem rather sad
So much has changed

It was songs of love that
I would sing to them
And I would memorize each word
Those old memories
Still sound so good to me
As they melt the years away

All my best memories
Come back to me
Some can even make me cry
It's yesterday once more......

My fate was sealed. There was no getting around it. If I was to do what I told Hartley I would do, then I had to prepare myself for the barrage of emotions I was about to encounter. The Boyz in the Grove were just ordinary people, but they had some real extraordinary stories.

A few days later, I found myself seated at the computer staring at the screen. My thoughts once again raced through

65

my mind. Where would I start? How could I tell these stories, on paper anyway? To my great surprise, once I had pecked out the first few words it all just kinda flowed along.

The best I know how, here are the stories that Jacob Hartley and I had stored up for over thirty years.

CHAPTER 1

You Gotta Get Started Somewhere

There are not exactly a lot of job opportunities for a long, lanky boy who wears his britches way on up past his belly button. You might call 'em hip waders. I was told the only way to get ahead is if you know somebody. I mean you have to have the right contacts to land any kinda job at thirteen. I knew just the right person, too. I mean I had me some big aspirations. I was going to save my money and buy me a moped (mo-ped). Just in case you never heard of a moped, it is a motor-scooter with bicycle-type wheels and you had to pedal it to crank it. It had a two-speed transmission and was about the size of a jumbo 28-inch bicycle. I could buy me one for one hundred fifty dollars.

My first job was not exactly with a Fortune Five Hundred company, but it was with a self-made man. This fellow had a gas station and a Laundromat. He hired me to work about ten hours every weekend at a whopping one buck an hour. All he wanted me to do was keep the trash picked up and give out change at the Laundromat. I thought it was great; I was all about customer service. That seemed like good money to me, because I had picked cotton for this guy for a nickel a pound. I don't believe I ever earned enough to even buy a Coke and a pack of crackers. A few weeks later, I got replaced at the Laundromat with a change machine. It didn't talk and it worked on. While I was working there, I looked on the bathroom walls and was surprised by what I saw.

Have you ever seen all the names on the bathroom walls? I figured I might get lucky so I called a few of the numbers. Every time a call was made, I got the phone hung up right in my ear. Why would they put their names on the wall if they didn't expect a call? Women, I don't guess we will ever figure them out.

There was something else I discovered during this time: cigarette machines. Those bad boys were forty-five cents a pack and if nobody was looking, I could put my money in and pull the handle. I started with Kool Filters, they had good commercials on TV. Besides, a lot of men that came in the station smoked them. I figured if they were good enough for them, they were good enough for me. I knew a couple of my buds in the Grove had already started puffing on some cancer sticks, and it was about time for me to prove I was tough. I didn't prove it, but I did feel cool. On the way home from a hard day at the Laundromat, I had to unwind. Once I got on my bike to head home, I would stop about a hundred and fifty yards from the store on the side of Jackson Highway and have me a smoke. There was a big concrete drainpipe that crossed under the highway and it was a good hiding place. It was probably five feet tall. Right there was where it all started. I had me a nasty habit real quick.

One thing I learned during my extensive career with laundry and money was this is a dog-eat-dog world. I mean there is competition in free enterprise. A fourteen-year-old boy ended up beating me out of my gas-pumping gig. It was not the end of the road, there must have been bigger things for me.

My first job was short-lived but I was determined to be self-reliant. I mean after all, I was almost fourteen. I knew I couldn't depend on the want ads so I had to rely on word of mouth.

Being a mature young buck, there had to be just the right job for me out there somewhere. Finally, Ms. Betty

Henderson from the church told Mama about something I might be interested in. Her husband, Clay Henderson Sr., owned the most famous catfish restaurant in Newton County. People from miles around knew about Henderson's fresh catfish. There was a possibility I could get a job as a busboy. Clay Jr., their son, and I were in Scouts together so again, I had an inside track. I landed that job and was well on the way to getting my moped. I didn't make but one dollar an hour but the waitress split tips with me.

There was another boy that worked as a busboy. His name was Wayne Shadburn and he lived down below the restaurant on Henderson Mill Road. Wayne's daddy was Jute Shadburn who was the best auto mechanic in three counties. His mama's name was Patsy. I really enjoyed working with Wayne and we ended up spending a lot of time together. Even though he didn't live in the Pecan Grove, he was still a pretty good boy and a good friend. Wayne had a Cushman scooter. It was red with a white and red seat. We would ride that thing down Henderson Mill Road like it was a Harley Davison. Sometimes, we could get up past forty-five miles per hour going down a hill. That encouraged me to work hard to get my first motorized vehicle.

I was kinda nervous, though, because I had never been in a restaurant before, much less worked at one. The first night a couple of the waitresses and Dale, the owner's oldest son, showed me what I was supposed to do. I was to clean off the tables and carry the dishes back to the kitchen. It sounded pretty simple, but there were several problems. One problem was that people started lining up about six thirty to get a catfish plate. That simply meant we better hustle if we didn't want to get hollered at. I worked hard and moved as fast as I could. There was another problem I noticed right away, though. As you started through the narrow kitchen you had better watch where you were going because it was very crowded. The floor was slick, too. Slinging all those fish, French fries, and hush puppies made that floor as slick as a baby's butt. Needless to say, I learned how to slip and slide without falling.

Those first few nights it felt like closing time would never come. All that running from the dining room to the kitchen like we were doing would wear out the best. I just knew once those doors locked, I could sit down and rest for a few minutes. But that was not the case, I mean there was still sweeping and mopping and cleaning to do. As I said, the waitresses did share some of the tips, and we all could sit down to a good meal once everything was done. I would usually get a ride home from Dale Henderson. I can remember one night in particular, I had got me a good plug of tobacco to chew while I was mopping and I just knew I could work faster. I had me a ham steak after all the cleaning was done and it was tasty. Dale called out and said, "Ricky, you 'bout ready?" Before I got into his car, I got me another plug.

When Dale found out I had tobacco in my mouth, he wouldn't let me spit all the way to the house. It was about a four-mile ride. I was green by the time I got out of the car. I ran to the bathroom and started puking my guts out. Mama and Daddy got up to see what was wrong. I told them it must have been the ham steak I had for supper. They never suspected that I had swallowed tobacco juice. That incident broke me completely from chewing, but my smoking habit was still there.

I must have worked at Henderson's a year or so. Anyway, there were people I met at fourteen that I still have fond memories of. There was Mammy who cooked most of the fish, and then there was Elaine, Ruth, Beverly, and Nita who all were waitresses. Nita was my cousin, and I remember when Jimmy Little would bring her to work in his Chevelle. The biggest reason I liked him was because he had such a nice car. They ended up getting married a year or two later.

Her name became Nita Little. Think about it, she caught some grief with that name.

I got my moped that summer and learned that hard work can pay off. I kept saving my money and was able to get a real motorcycle later.

Working at Henderson's and coming home smelling like grease was just the beginning of my work experiences but quite a memorable one. I am reminded of those days now, every time I go into the Waffle House.

I had several different jobs during my high school years, besides Henderson's. My next favorite occupation was working at Ramsey Furniture Company. I was sixteen when I started there and C.D. and Sam Ramsey owned the place. Biff Hutchinson and I were delivery boys. We had a ball and gave that old delivery truck pure hell. I remember Mr. Ramsey asking us one day if we were abusing his furniture truck because he had already had to replace the clutch twice in six months. That place had been in business since 1919, the same year my daddy was born. I believed Mr. C.D. may have started it. We always talked about having a bronze statue of him being put at the front of the store. We even hid *Playboy magazines under the seat of the delivery truck. Of course we got caught and vehemently denied knowing anything about such trash. If I could live it over, I'm not sure I would change a thing.*

CHAPTER 2

Lowest Man on the Totem Pole

Being an eighth grader at E.L. Ficquett School was the highest honor a student could posses. Jacob Harley and Ricky Darby were El Supremo in May of '69. I mean, we were the seniors of grammar school and those other students had better respect that. The problem with all that was, our kingdom was about to crumble. Our summer break was awesome. I worked some at my first job and in June, turned fourteen; we seemed to have it going on. Suddenly, the harsh reality set in. We were about to be freshmen, also known as "fresh meat."

Newton County High School would be a brand-new life to most of us. We would meet students from all over the county. They would be coming from Porterdale, Oxford, Mansfield, and Newborn. I had already heard about some of them boys from Porterdale, too. If that was not enough, the all-black high school would merge with us for the first time. Some folks say the Lord ain't gonna put more on you than you can bear. I was having serious doubts about that in September of '69. We had heard there would be picketers in front of the school because of this thing called "desegregation."

Well, when I got to school on the first day, there were no picketers but there were a lot of strange new faces, all shapes and sizes. The first time I walked down the halls, I said to myself, "I will get lost in this place and never find all my classes." I went one way and Jacob went the other to homeroom. Our new high school teachers briefed us on what to expect, gave us a brief overview of the facility, and handed us our schedules. The intercom came on and our new principal welcomed everyone, we had the pledge to the flag, a couple of announcements, and on to our first class we were headed.

I wound my way around the building and found my first class. Low and behold, Jacob and another friend from Ficquett were in the class with me in that room, too. I did notice several of the opposite sex that didn't look to bad. (This high school thing might not be all that bad after all.)

Our locker numbers had been assigned earlier and by the end of the day, I knew I would need to find mine. What I didn't know was that the senior boys already knew where all the freshman lockers were. (I think I mentioned something about "fresh meat" already.) When I loaded up my locker with some of my new books, I was met by a clan of seniors. The first thing I heard was "Time for initiation, fresh meat." Every one of them had their senior rings turned around and started bopping me in the head. I thought I would have a concussion before they got through. My head looked like a scrub board but I was not about to wash any clothes. I just wanted a Bayer aspirin.

Another thing I noticed pretty quickly was that we were about to enter a field of higher learning. Some of the classes we would take our folks knew very little about. When I got home, I told Mama and Daddy how smart I would become. They didn't seem to take that very well. They even told me I was not half as smart as I thought I was. I didn't want to argue, but I could see they did not appreciate my comment.

Every night, I had to sit down and watch the news. Huntley and Brinkley always brought some of the most graphic scenes from home and abroad. The Vietnam war was still in full swing and it even hit home. Some of the boys from Covington were coming home in body bags. Then there were flag burners and war protesters here in the States. The duo gave live coverage of Neil Armstrong as he made his first steps on the moon. Then they showed the mass of people at the orgy, dope-smoking concert called Woodstock. We never missed the news and I will never forget the closing words from this elite news team. "Good night, Chet. Good night, David, and good night for NBC News."

Locally, we had begun to see some protesting from the black community about desegregation. They marched in front of the high school holding picket signs and chanting. Sometimes, they would sing some old Negro spirituals. On the other side of town, the Grand of the Knights, aka the KKK, were having a rally of their own. They had their ideas and were trying to convince all the white people that they were right. My daddy had some real narrow views on how things ought to shake out. I was really a little confused about the whole thing.

With all the news, there was still a lot going on that would never get national coverage or even local attention. I am referring to the grapevine and eyewitness accounts from the halls of Newton County High School. I'll be honest with you; it was a lot more exciting than some of the things I had watched on TV and most of this stuff you could see firsthand. I begin to be privy to some information after the third or fourth month at the new school.

You would walk in the boys' bathroom to pee and one of the male teachers would already be inside. They had usually caught two or three students smoking in the boys' room. I believe there was even a song written about that. Sometimes, you could catch some real action when one of the studly football players had been caught cheatin' on his cheerleader girlfriend. She would throw his lettered jacket in his face just after she had slapped the crap out of him. He might have been a star on the field, but at that point, he was lower than a snake's belly. You could also witness a good fight in the hall every once in a while. The best fights were between girls. I mean you could see elbows slinging, hair flying, and panties showin'. It was better than anything you could see at the movies.

Even though freshmen were the lowest on the totem pole, it was obvious you gotta start somewhere. Jacob and I had most of our classes together and he built a reputation for being fairly tough. He was not afraid of scrappin' and would welcome a chance to prove it. I felt like I was sprouting wings because there seemed to be a newfound freedom I had not known before. We were in the era of peace and love and I was all about the love part. My new friends from all around shared the same enthusiasm. We had arrived at a new plateau, a precipice of sorts. I could see how the adults in our lives could not appreciate it. After all, you must experience it to know it. Bottom line: we were getting smarter than our folks. They had to understand we were growing up very rapidly.

There was one problem. My mama just could not get all of this for the life of her. She had turned into a different person. She would NOT listen to me. She refused to allow me to experience the freedom I deserved. She had the nerve to tell me I was rebellious. If anyone was rebellious, it was her. I just thought differently. Our relationship was a lot like oil and water; it just didn't mix very well. There was this one time we had a knock-down drag-out and Mama slapped me. Well, not even thinking, I slapped her back. All she said was, "I AM GONNA LET YOUR DADDY DEAL WITH YOU, BOY."

When Daddy walked in the door, Mama cornered him and explained a much different story than I remember. He called me over, I was sure we could work this out like two mature adults. When I started to open my mouth, Daddy surprised me. He said, "Boy, you best just shut the hell up." He then commenced to grab me by my collar and stand me up against the wall. Well, my feet were not exactly touching the floor either. He looked me square in the eyes and said these echoing words, "Boy, if you ever lay a hand on your mama again, I will stomp your ass. You want to be a man, I will treat you like one. This is my wife you are messing with and I WILL deal with you if it ever happens again. You got me?"

As soon as I got my heart out of my throat, the only answer I could come up with was, "YESSS, SIR!"

IT WOULD HAVE BEEN SO MUCH EASIER IF THEY COULD HAVE JUST UNDERSTOOD THE COMPLEXITY OF A FRESHMAN.

CHAPTER 3

A Studebaker Truck and Wide-open Spaces

The Pecan Grove was not exactly a place to start a farm. All the lots were less than an acre and we lived fairly close to each other. The Cooks gave several people permission to use the land right behind their house and some of the folks took advantage of that.

Brent's daddy, John, used it to raise quail and chickens and have a family garden. He tried his hand at farming, too. He dug out a watering hole and got a few head of cows. John eventually bought that spot of land. There was another family that started some serious farming. Blue Hartley built a couple of barns, fenced in about a half acre, and started getting animals. He bought goats, chickens, a small horse, and a pony. It was not long before the animals outgrew the area. Blue was getting prepared to expand his venture when he bought a farm truck. He found a 1950 Studebaker pickup. It was dark blue and rusted, you could see daylight through the floorboard, but it ran like a sewing machine.

The first place they moved the animals was behind their house and through the woods. There was an old home place that had been abandoned for years. It was part of the Cook property, too. There was an old rundown barn that looked like it had never seen a coat of paint. You could see the worn field rocks used for the foundation of an old house. The hand-dug well was next to where the house used to sit. You might have to drop a bucket in the old well but it had some cold water. I saw the longest black snake ever next to that well. That thing 'bout got the best of me.

Jacob learned to drive in that old truck in no time flat. It had a four-speed; that meant three speeds forward, one speed backwards, and a granny gear. It was not long before Jacob was popping the clutch and cutting circles. Before long, I was riding with him to feed the animals and check the pastures. At least a couple of times a week, the animals were getting out of the fence and everybody was trying to find 'em and see where they broke through. The fences were in a whole lot worse shape than Blue thought they were. Every time you fixed one gap, two more would appear. Blue finally just got fed up.

The animals had to be moved so Blue made a deal with Grady Crawford to rent his pasture. Grady Crawford was a household name to the people in the Pecan Grove. I think he had lived where he was since before Sherman came through. He had inherited over one hundred acres; most of it was across the road from the Pecan Grove. His house was a rough-looking place and very few people had been inside. Grady had a habit of drinking too much and we were afraid he might shoot us if we tried lookin' in. I always heard he had a bunch of antiques; don't guess I'll ever know. He did have an old 8N Ford tractor and several acres of cotton, but I don't know if he made a living selling cotton. There was even an old sharecropper's house across the road from us. Anyway, he was getting up in age and renting the pasture would give him a little more income and help keep the property up at the same time.

These pastures were in a lot better shape than the others and they got in top-notch shape pretty quickly. Jacob had to cross the road now to get to the pasture and drive right up next to Grady's house to open the gate. I became the world's fastest gate opener. There were wide-open spaces in that pasture and you could ride about the entire pasture in the truck. It wasn't very long before we found out we could ford the creek and cross the pasture and end up over on East End Road, which was our ticket to freedom.

We had big plans. If everything worked out like we thought, Jacob could see his newfound romance on the north end of the county. The ride was about twelve miles one way. He could even drop me off if I could find a girl around the back side of Oxford. This gal Jacob had fallen for was originally from Germany. I had always heard German girls were real hot. I found me a red-headed beauty right outside Oxford, so things seemed to be working out.

Jacob had a friend whose uncle ran the Loop 81 Shell Station. We would stop off there and get a couple of dollars worth of gas and a snack. That station was where we heard about rum-flavored cigars. We could buy a pack of cigarettes, too. I had done "swore off" chewing tobacco after my unpleasant experience earlier. Only real men could smoke rum-flavored cigars anyway.

I bet we put 10,000 miles on that old truck just sneaking around. If there was a dirt road within twenty miles, we would ride it. We just knew we couldn't go anywhere our folks might see us. You just might say we had a "covert operation" going.

We even discovered the Rock Quarry off Dearing Road. There were all sorts of stories about that place. It had been a granite quarry in years past. One story goes that it is several hundred feet deep and when they hit water, they couldn't get the equipment out in time. It was also told there were several stolen vehicles in the bottom. That story did prove credible years later. There was about a twenty-five-foot rock cliff and that was the place Joe Heard and some of the football players would dive off into the water. About every year, the rescue squad was retrieving a body out of that old quarry.

I get to thinking about all that now. It's just a wonder nothing bad ever happened to us. That ol' truck never ran hot, never had a flat tire, the law never jumped us. I reckon the good Lord was just looking out after us.

I wish teenagers today could experience some of the stuff I did back then; riding through the creek and water soaking your feet because of the hole in the floorboard, smelling manure and honeysuckle at the same time, or getting some "real" water with an old bucket out of a hand-dug well. Nothing can ever replace what we experienced in that old Studebaker.

CHAPTER 4

Paintin' the Town....I Might Add, Without Success

One of the favorite pastimes for a lot of the kids about my age was to visit the Strand Theatre. It was on the square in downtown Covington right next to Covington Furniture. I would try and talk Mama and Daddy into letting me go about twice or maybe three times a month. That was until Jacob got his driver's license and then I could go 'bout every week. Sometimes, I would meet a girl there, or at least try and hook up. It just didn't happen as often as I would have liked. All this sounded like a good idea but remember, this romancing thing was pretty new to me. I could always hope beyond hope and sometimes got lucky. I mean you could walk down that dark aisle and get plum jealous, seeing some of your best friends caught up in the heat of the moment.

Nobody ever said, "Are you going to the movie theatre this weekend?" We were from Covington, Georgia and that was way too proper for us. Somebody would say, "You going to the show Friday night?" One of the people who then ran the Strand also worked at the Hub Drive-In. We always called him the Bingo man. The reason for that was they had Bingo at the Hub several nights a week and during the intermission, he called out the numbers. I don't remember his name, but I believe he was on Thorazine. I mean you would about fall asleep while he was calling out the numbers. You have seen others that way; they are so dry that when they tell you their name you start yawning.

There is always something different about the smell of the picture show, too. Today, you can smell fresh popcorn and you know where you are. Then it was the mixture of machinery, old reel to reels, cigarette smoke, popcorn, and a not-so-clean bathroom. That stinks, right? No, that smell today would almost be nostalgic to those who remember.

Well, this story takes place on what was just another typical Friday night, but this time, instead of going to the movie, we would go down to the drugstore. I got me a milkshake and a pack of Salem cigarettes. Jacob and I and a couple of others decided we would just walk around town. We walked over to Allen's Five and Dime, where David Barker worked. He told us he would be off in about thirty minutes and if we would wait on him, we could have a real good time. I figured maybe he had some liquor stashed or he knew of a real hot girl.

David had a different idea of a real good time. When he came out of the store, he had something hidden under his coat. All of us were inquisitive. "Whatcha got, man?" was the question we all had.

I was thinking, I hope he ain't done robbed that place. Well, he pulled out two extra large spray cans of fluorescent orange paint.

He said, "Tonight, boys, we are going to paint the town."

I was not sure what he had in mind but I was game, as well as all the rest of us. There were about six of us "juvenile delinquents" that night.

We all started walking and painting. We would change a thirty-five-mile-an-hour speed limit sign to eighty-five miles an hour. We painted car tags orange and mailboxes. But up to this time, I still hadn't touched a can of paint and didn't the rest of the night. Things were about to get real interesting, though.

As we walked out of town, down Conyers Street, we decided to head over toward the schools and the Board of Education Building. I mean, during all this time, we were laughing and talking and smoking. I was having a pretty good time. I did kinda wonder what we would do over at the school. E.L. Ficquett Grammar School, Newton County High School, and The Board of Education were all within spittin' distance of one another. During that time, Whitlow Richardson was the school superintendent. I don't guess any of us had ever met the man personally. We heard talk of him and all our folks knew him. Somehow, all of us knew we were supposed to hate the school superintendent, though. I still don't know where that came from, but it didn't matter for us. We were on a mission.

By this time, quite a few things were glow-in-the-dark orange. What we were about to do should have been recorded somewhere on the walls in the Dumbest Acts Hall of Fame Museum. Suddenly, one of us had the bright idea that we should write on the side of the Board of Education building. So in huge, glow-in-the-dark orange paint, we wrote, "WHITLOW SUX" and "DOWN WITH RICHARDSON." A couple of the guys thought it was a real work of art. I thought it was just a pretty dumb idea, but I was along for the fun. We finished up a can of paint and we promising young artists headed toward the Loop.

We figured we could get over to the Shell Station on Loop 81 and back before the show ended. We could get some more cigarettes, a pack of rum cigars, a bottled Coke, and a pack of cheese crackers when we got there. Out Newton Drive, we went over toward Highway 278 and then straight to Loop 81. It was a pretty good haul, but we were paintin' the town, we could make it. We painted stop signs, the highway, and the I-20-Loop 81 bridge before we totally ran out of paint. We hid when cars came by so nobody would ever see us, we thought...

There were two people you never wanted to cross up with in Newton County during that time. Of course, you know there were more than two, but stay with me here. Mr. Jim Bohannan was the truant officer and Mr. Wendell Kitchens was the juvenile man.

I feared both these men. They could easily send me to reform school and I had no intentions of going there. You probably done guessed it, by Monday morning, we were caught. Mr. Bohannan, who worked for the school board had sniffed around and found out who was responsible for paintin' the town. We were in the principal's office with our folks by close of school on Monday. I was already scared to death but Mr. Bohannan put the fear of God in me. He said, "Boys, you've got forty-eight hours to get all the orange paint up. If it's not done, I call Mr. Kitchens." I have never scrubbed so hard in my life. We used paint thinner and Brillo pads. In forty-eight hours, he didn't see any orange paint shinin' anywhere.

I reckon that was the closest I ever came to being sent to reform school. I could see me walking down the hall with big, burly guards pulling a ball and chain. That ain't even funny to think about, but some of the other boys weren't even fazed. This could just be the beginning of their illegal activity.

CHAPTER 5

Motorcycle Rides and Running From the Law

As you know, one of my dreams was to get a real motorcycle. My daddy finally went over to Sears-Roebuck and found a one-hundred-twenty-five-CC, two-stroke street bike. During that time, you could buy about anything at Sears. I hear they had building supplies so you could even buy the kitchen sink at Sears. This motorcycle was fire-engine red with a smooth black leather seat; it had shiny chrome fenders and two chrome pipes coming out from under the frame. It was pretty slick but was not exactly what I had in mind. As fate would have it, the guts to the muffler wouldn't stay in and it only ran about fifty percent of the time. It sounded like a chainsaw off a pulpwood truck when the guts popped out. There were no lemon laws back then, but some places would just give you a refund if you got a dud. So Sears refunded Daddy the money since he was such a good customer. Once we got that straightened out, we went to Pratt-Dudley Building Supply, who also sold Honda motorcycles. David Dodd showed me and Daddy just the right bike. It was a 1970 Honda 175 off-road motorcycle. That thing was a beast, orange with tall fenders and off-road tires; it had a four-cycle engine so you didn't have to mix the gas and oil. It even had electric start. I was set; I

could watch Evil Kinevil on TV and learn cool tricks to
impress everybody in the neighborhood. That was my intent
anyway.

Several months later, Brent's dad bought him a Kawasaki
125; it was a dirt bike, too, but his was purple and a two-
stroke. It was quite a while later that Jacob's daddy got him
a Honda 175 kinda like mine, only newer and lighter.

Anyway, for a good long while, it was mostly just me
and Brent riding. We made trails where there were no trails
and found dirt roads we had never been on. Actually, some
of these roads were old pulpwood trails. We ventured out
a little, too. This was about the same time Alcovy Trailer
Park was being built. Trailer parks and the sixties and early
seventies were words that were synonymous. Brent and
I checked out the new road leading into the trailer park
because it was just about directly across the road from his
house. It dumped out onto East End Road almost at the creek
bridge. East End Road, you have already heard about because
it was mine and Jacob's escape route to freedom when we
were in the Studebaker. You see things a lot differently on
two wheels than you do four. I mean, it can get up close
and personal. A rabbit or possum runs across the road in
a car, you don't sweat at all. On a motorcycle, let's just say
it tightens muscles that only get tightened when you are
scared. I used to call that the sphincter factor.

Other things having a motorcycle will do for you ain't
so bad. It will make the worst sort of geek cool, and it is a
girl magnet, too. I ain't found a girl yet that didn't want to
feel the wind blow through her clothes and let her hair blow
in the breeze. Of course, up to that time, I had never asked
any either. Next door to Jacob was where Velma Anderson
lived. She was a real country woman who was raisin' her
three kids alone. Her husband left her and didn't do right
by her according to some folk. She lived a little differently
from most of us, or at least I thought so. She was the first

woman I ever saw breastfeed a child. I mean, I thought that child would stop after six months or so but I believe he had been walkin' awhile before she ever weaned him. It seemed like he wouldn't stop before kindergarten. A mama dog just pushes her young away but that was not the case here. Oh yeah, she could hoe a garden better than most men and she always had a dip of snuff in her lower gum. I guess you would call her salt of the earth now.

Anyway, two of her nieces started spending time with her to help out. I believe it was her brother's daughter and stepdaughter. Bonnie and Frankie were about a couple of years older than Brent and me and they were from out of town, Stone Mountain, Georgia. Let's just say, Brent and I got to be like a couple of dogs in heat when these girls were around. In case you ain't from my neck of the woods, let me do a little explaining. When a male dog found a female dog that was ready to breed, you couldn't run the male dog off with a stick. You could yell, throw rocks, or even shoot at that ol' dog and he would still come back. I don't reckon we were quite that bad, but we were pretty persistent. I mean, these were two "older women" from out of town, and we were not about to miss our chance. After some serious courting, we both found ourselves going steady. Bonnie became my girl and Frankie was Brent's. Of course, I thought Bonnie was the prettier of the two. She had dark brown, shoulder-length hair that kinda flipped up in the back. She was a little shorter than me but was well proportioned. Frankie was a little taller and slimmer and had wavy, long brown hair. She had a pretty good overbite, too, but that was no problem.

Now that I think about it a little bit, going steady may have not been proper terminology. We had some real good times riding those girls around the neighborhood on the back of our motorcycles. We even took 'em back to Earnest and Mammy's to do some serious lovin' but their will was a lot stronger than ours. Still, there ain't nothing like having a girl hugged up to your back while bugs are stickin' to your teeth since you can't quit smiling.

We met a lot of people while we were out riding. After Alcovy Trailer Park was developed, Brent and I met two of the first residents. They were Steve and Steve; that is, Steve Nelms and Stevie Garrison. Stevie Garrison always made motorcycle noises when we came up. They were best friends and recently married their high school sweethearts. Both of them knew my brother, Larry, so we had something to talk about. These guys just seemed to encourage the daredevil in us. Anyway, from that point on, we seemed to venture out further and further. We figured as long as we didn't get caught, we would stretch our limits.

As you already have heard, we were able to find some spots that would have never been discovered without us venturing out a little further each time we got out. We found an old abandoned home place with a lake and wild roses. It was as pretty as a picture before whoever owned it left. It might have even inspired the painter Thomas Kinkaid. We all liked it so much we called it Paradise. Then we found the road to the Rock Quarry, where all the high school football players and their girls hung out. Well, you have already heard about that once but the plot thickens a little right here so just bear with me. If you hung a right at the turn to the Rock Quarry, you ended up at Highway 278 just across from the Cow Palace. Then, if you just went a little further, there was Loop 81. That was where the Shell Station was. Loop 81 Shell was a busy place because it was just off I-20. I could buy cigarettes out of a machine or get rum-flavored cigars. The real reason I am telling about these places ain't because they are so cool, but to let you see that if you are not careful, before you know it, you find yourself places a boy without a driver's license has no business being. As long as we were staying close to home and on the old pulpwood roads, we were safe. We just couldn't do it, though; we just had to venture out.

Every day I rode, I got a little braver, until getting on the highway meant nothing. It did mean something to the men in blue, though. There were a few of those Covington Police who just seemed to watch for us. I would sneak up to Highway 278 and watch for the cops and then dart across to the Cow Palace. I mean, that was the hangout for all the cool folks. They had jukeboxes and a dance floor. It was a drive-in kinda like a Sonic today for you, the younger readers. The Cow Palace is the first place I ever ate a pizza sandwich or homemade onion rings. Anyway, Brent and I were leaving the Cow Palace one day and had just got across 278 when a cop spotted us. I saw him turn around once we had hit the dirt road. I looked at Brent and he looked at me. At about the same time, we both downshifted and opened the throttle. All I could see was dust and blue lights in a distance. We figured if we stayed on the dirt road, we could get away. That close call 'bout scared the crap out of me, and we talked about "outrunning the law" for months. Thinking about it now, though, I think that old cop was just playing with us. I mean think about it, a Honda 175 and a Kawasaki 100 outrunning a Plymouth Fury with a 440 magnum engine. That was not very likely, but it does make a good story, don't it?

CHAPTER 6

Pickups and Motorcycles
Just Don't Mix

Most everybody who has ever ridden on a dirt road knows you drive right down the middle of the road unless you meet a car. Those old dirt roads had become real familiar to me. I had dodged deer and rabbit as well as an occasional vehicle. You could really stir up dust, too. When it rained, those roads got extra slick and I tried not to get on 'um after a fresh rain. You could ruin a pair of wrangler blue jeans with that old Georgia red mud. Besides that, I didn't want to end up in the ditch, because I just was not strong enough to pull that bike out by myself.

Jacob hadn't got his motorcycle yet so he would ride with me from time to time. I guess it was payback from the Studebaker days. We would sneak over to Loop 81 Shell and buy some rum cigars or a couple of packs of cigarettes. There were a couple of buddies we would meet over there sometimes and we would even tell lies about the night we painted the town. There was one day, though, that still stands out in my mind. I mean we all have days that we will probably never forget, right?

We left the house right after school, put on our helmets, and off we went. We cut through Alcovy Trailer Park and hung a right on East End Road over the tracks and over onto

Dearing Road. I can still almost smell Sam Hay's Dairy. There was always an encounter of that fresh smell. I am not saying it was a pleasant smell, but it was fresh. You never knew what aroma you would encounter, maybe sour corn silage or fresh cow manure. That odor caused me to always want to get by that place in a real hurry. This day was no different.

The road leading to the dairy went up a hill then you topped the rise. As you went past the dairy, the home place was on the right and just below it was another little rise. You couldn't see over the rise so you just had to take a chance of another car coming. I guess I had been up and down that road a hundred times and never meet another vehicle. I just figured I never would. How wrong I was this time, though. I did slow down a little because Jacob was on the back. When I topped that rise, I saw a pickup truck headed right toward me. I veered to the left and it looked like he was headed straight for me so I started to move to the right. I thought we just might make it, but we didn't. Some how or another, I hit the left side of the bed of that truck. About that time, Jacob went airborne. I went under the truck and came out past the back bumper. I was no Evil Kenevil that day. I was real lucky, though. The old man driving the truck jumped out and came running to me, not even seeing Jacob yet. He said, "Boy, are you alright?"

Before I could say a word, I started screaming for my friend. He was out cold and I thought I had done killed him. He was lying in that ditch with his helmet still on and not moving an inch. I couldn't think about me, I was too scared. Besides, how would I ever explain this one? Was I going to jail? Would I be grounded for life? Would Jacob come to? My mind was racing. Thankfully, in just a couple of minutes, Jacob started to come around. About the time I got to the ditch where my buddy was lying, I fell slap to the ground and my leg was killing me. I was sick as a dog, when a saw what was left of my Honda. I think the old man driving the truck thought I was faking at first but he figured out quickly I was in real pain. He smelled like he had probably been nipping at the bottle a little, so the law was never called.

That old fellow got my motorcycle in the back of his pickup and took me and Jacob to the house. I was hurting something serious. I figured I must have broken something in my leg.

We got to the house and the old guy helped me in, as I hobbled on one foot. I thought I would never get up those two steps from the carport to the kitchen. Daddy was already home and instantly recognized the man I had collided with. The fellow worked as a salesman at Ginn Motor Company. Of course, Daddy had known him for years. He gave Daddy his side of the story and was on his way, no cops, no ambulance, and no insurance. I believe Daddy was more worried about me than whether the man was drunk or whether my motorcycle could be fixed. Of course, Mama's first words were, "I knew that thing was gonna half kill you; don't plan on ever riding it again." That brought me real comfort. After all, she was the one with all the compassion.

Daddy loaded me up and took me to Newton County Hospital Emergency Room. We were met by Dr. Callaway, our family doctor. He shot me on back to X-ray and they discovered my foot and the bottom part of my leg were broken. I didn't need X-rays for that, I could have told them and probably saved that expense!

When everything was said and done, I had a cast up to my knee and crutches to get around on. I do remember getting some real powerful pain meds, too. I mean that stuff took away all my worries. It wasn't very long before I had to learn to use those crutches. If you have ever used 'em you know there are some do's and don'ts to walking with crutches. I had to learn all that on my own because as you know, there are no instructions with those things. School books, crowded hallways, and stairs were another story in itself. I made it, though, with a little help from my friends.

About six weeks later, the cast was off and the motorcycle was repaired. I was once again ready to ride off into the wild blue yonder but not without apprehension and argument from Mama. I was ready for yet another great adventure.

CHAPTER 7

Fast Cars and Fine Women

The inevitable finally comes in the life of parents: Their sons get their driver's licenses. This was the case with Blue and Larue. Jacob had his license and Blue let his boy drive the red '64 Galaxie 500 that he had been driving back and forth to work for a good many years. This was a fine car, a two-door hard top, red on red with a 390 engine and three on the tree. The old car would take you on down the road, too. We had snuck around in the Studebaker and been all over the county, but now we were legal; well, Jacob was. That did seem to make a difference when it came to speed and mischief. We could ride through the Cow Palace legally and Jacob could dump the clutch and light up the tires. Now, when we sped, at least he knew we might get a ticket and get sent on our way. The Ford would hang a curve a lot better than the old farm truck did.

Every once in a while, Jacob would find somebody who wanted to race. It was nothing like street racing today, and it was not always a quarter-mile run either. He would start at fifty or sixty miles an hour sometimes and race about a half mile or so. I will tell you, the Ford was not the fastest thing in the area but it was competitive. I remember one race with Lanier Johnson. He drove a '62 Impala with a 283. Lanier lived over on Piper Road about three or four miles from the Pecan Grove. He and Jacob got to jawing back and forth about who had the fastest car, until they come up with a little wager. I can't even remember what the wager was now, but I do remember where the race would be. They were gonna go right outside Oxford on Highway 81 and pick a spot. Well, they found it just before you got to Womack's old store. They would race past Jim McCart's station and as they started up the hill, the race would end and a winner would be declared. It doesn't always work exactly like you plan, but this one was pretty close. They were rolling along about forty miles an hour and stomped it. Jacob shoved the Ford back up in second gear and away we went. At about seventy-five or eighty, he dropped it in third and Lanier was just six or seven feet in front. I mean this was a close race, but when we came down the hill at McCart's store, Lanier got the lead and outran us by a little less than a car length. Jacob was so mad he was ready to fight and that would have been something else to see, too. After some choice language and beating on the steering wheel, we both figured we had better things to do than fight. Besides, that would not have done any good anyway.

There were some real cars back then. You would pay forty or fifty thousand dollars today for cars that sold for less than $4000 brand-spankin'-new during our time. You could buy a sweet, fast car for less than $1500 back then. We had made a lot of friends around and met a lot of guys with hot, hot cars. I remember a fellow we met at Anderson's Service Station. He had a Dodge Challenger with a 426 Hemi. People would gather round and make bets. They set up a Coke bottle and he would dump the clutch and the front tires would jump off the ground enough to jump the Coke bottle. My palms get sweaty thinking about all that. You would have a hard time imagining all this unless you lived it. I ain't seen nothing like it since.

An old boy named Tony Pippin hung around at the station all the time. If I remember correctly, he worked part-time changing tires and doin' some light mechanic work. He had a '66 SS 396 Chevelle. Tony drove that car hard, but it was one of the fastest around. He let me drive it one day. I was just fifteen. He told me I could drive it down the road but I'd better not tear it up. Well, I got down the road a little ways and punched it a little and punched it a little more. I turned around and headed back and when I tried to shift into second gear, it wouldn't go. I was sweating bullets afraid of what Tony might do to me. The truth was the car was about ragged out already. It was a wonder the thing even ran the way Tony had driven it. I got back to the service station and told him what happened; he never let on like anything was wrong with the car. I told him I would save my money and pay whatever it cost to fix it. He told me, "Well, you will have two years to save up your money because I am going to basic training in two weeks."

After basic training, Tony was shipped to Vietnam. Everybody around was worried about all the boys from Covington. I heard about eight or ten months after Tony was shipped out that he got shot out of a helicopter and was killed on enemy soil. You might guess, I never got to pay for the transmission. His girlfriend eventually was given the car, but it never was the same. She ended up having it painted another color, put a smaller engine in it, and put in an automatic transmission. It was pretty obvious she was not interested in a hot rod.

It is so easy to get off on fast cars and street racing that you lose track of where you were going. I did name this chapter "Fast Cars and Fine Women," so I need to give the fine women equal play.

I don't think I mentioned it yet, but as a sophomore, I had me a senior girlfriend. Now let me tell you, that is worth you remembering. You gotta be stepping in high cotton when you are able to snag an older, more mature woman. One who has began to understand the finer things of life. I can see her now, with that long, flowing black hair and those beautiful eyes, her soft skin, and well, I had better stop while I am ahead because I really don't remember thinking any of that stuff. It does make it sound a little romantic, though. Donna was an outgoing, friendly girl who was not stuck on being a senior. She really did have a great personality. Any guys reading are already thinking about some of your buddies' description of a girl you never met. Your so-called friends' first descriptive words are "She has a great personality." Usually, those girls had to put a bone around their necks to get the dog to play with them. I know somebody's got to love 'em, just not me, at fifteen. So let me clarify, THIS GAL WAS PRETTY FINE.

There was one minor problem that you already know about. I couldn't drive legally. That is where Jacob came to the rescue. My folks gave me permission to see my new budding love, but her folks were the cautious type. They wanted us to stay at her house until they got to know me. That worked out better than you think. Jacob would drop me off in Covington Mill at Donna's and then he would head over toward Collum Road to see Dinah, his main squeeze at the time. Usually about 10:30, he would come by and pick me back up and we would head to the house.

Things have changed a lot since then, because we would sit in the living room and watch the little black-and-white television and make out the best we could. Most of the time, her mama and daddy were in the other room and we had to listen very, very carefully. Donna's sister was attending Wesleyan College and would come in a lot of times during our date. (Well, if that is what you want to call it.) We just never experienced any real quality time and that probably ain't really so bad. We had this arrangement for several months and of course, after a while, I guess she wised up

100

or maybe saw we were going nowhere fast. She might have gotten tired of watching Red Skelton or *Dialing for Dollars.* At any rate, I found myself a single man again. Those wild, raging hormones were ready to hunt and conquer the next prey; well, that is probably putting it a little strong. What I meant to say was, "I'll grovel and beg and give my biggest smile and maybe some girl will, at least, give me the time of day." At least that was my thinking at the time.

Jacob and I did do some double dating after I split up with Donna. I know Jacob was always with Dinah and if I remember right, I dated a couple of other girls but I don't want to mention names to protect the innocent. That is actually a way to avoid telling that I just don't remember who they were. I don't mean to hurt anybody but there has been a lot of water under the bridge since then. I was looking through my high school annual to try and jog my memory. I saw a lot of girls I thought I might have dated but I suspect several were just wishful thinking.

I can't tell you I ever had my way with a girl in the backseat of that old Ford, but I can say we had a lot of fun dreaming about it. I do remember riding through the old dirt road and crossing the haunted double bridges. The story was people had been murdered on the bridge and their spirits and the murderer's spirit still haunted the place. Every girl who ever went through there with me got so close I'd get to sweating. Jacob would stop on the first bridge and then spin off at the second bridge.

I don't know if I would ever want to relive those days, but it sure is neat to think about all of our silly antics thirty-five years later.

CHAPTER 8

Sophomore Seventy

As you can see, I had two major accomplishments under my belt: first dating experience and street racing (during my sophomore year at Newton High). I guess I want to change directions now and tell you a little more about my sophomore year and a lot more about 1970.

Brent was a freshman, but during that time, the eighth and ninth graders had to go to R.L. Cousins School. At one time, Cousins had been an all-black high school on the other end of town. After a year of fixin' up, it became the middle school as we know it today. Mr. Homer Sharp became the director of secondary education. He had been the high school principal for a long time. I guess it was time for him to start moving up. Coach Mac and Dr. Tinsley were co-principals at the high school. It was our first time to have a black principal. I got to know Dr. Tinsley firsthand, too. He was a real good man and seemed to really care about the students. Coach Mac had been a football coach and he didn't play around. He would put the fear of God in you. Here is how our high school annual described our co-principals:

Where you find the need of two strong, determined men with a helping hand, you'll find our co-principals, Mr. Tinsley and Mr. McLaney. Both of these men work for the betterment of Newton County High School. They are constantly busy making sure the school is clean and in order. Have you ever seen Mr. Tinsley or Mr. McLaney standing around? They aren't just standing there. The wheels in their minds are turning round and round trying to solve another problem.

A lot of things were going on that year and not just at our school. I would listen to the national news with Huntley and Brinkley every night. Richard Nixon was president of the United States and our troops were still in Vietnam. This was the year they would invade Cambodia. It was also the year 50,000 people in Peru were killed because of an earthquake. One of the saddest things was that it was the year the Beatles broke up and went their separate ways. How could I forget? It was also the year Janis Joplin and Jimmi Hendrix died from drug overdoses. They were both twenty-seven years old. The Carpenters, Simon and Garfunkel, and Blood, Sweat, and Tears were all hot bands at the time. Joe South made the song "Games People Play" a hit number one on the charts. We would hear Flip Wilson tell us every week, "The devil made me do it." It was the same year four Kent State students were killed by the National Guard. They were protesting against the war.

It was my second year of high school and I had made several new friends and began to build some unusual relationships. I had very little interest in my education, but I did want to have some fun. At fifteen, there were a lot of things I had not yet experienced. If I could get the right classes, it could help me accomplish some of my personal goals at the time. I am sure students today would never dream of trying to manipulate their schedules like we did in 1970 just to have a class with some hot new chic at school or even to hang with some buds. That would never happen today, I am sure of it.

Well, I remember I had to have English, math, a science, P.E., and a couple of electives. One of my electives was economics. I was also in the F.F.A. even though I had no intention of ever farming.

My reasoning for joining up was because some of my friends were involved and the real men were in F.F.A., well, except for one girl. Debbie Carroccino was the only female member because of her boyfriend if I remember right. None of us minded either because she happened to be one of the prettiest girls in the school. Some of my buds like Freddie, Andy, Ernie, and Stanley were in the club, too.

Mr. Barrow was our vocational ag. teacher. He lived down Highway 213 close to the house and was a pretty cool teacher. Miss Bradley was my English teacher. I remember her because she asked me not to bring my rubber snake back to school. Coach Fisher was my P.E. coach and also the football coach. Let me just say, he was all about football. The other teacher that stands out in my mind was Mr. Chambers, my algebra teacher.

To be honest, I only took algebra because I figured I would have to have it if I was planning on going to college. Jacob decided he would take it, too. Before I go any further, I need to tell you a little bit about the teacher. Mr. Chambers was probably in his late twenties or early thirties, but looked a little older because his hair was already turning gray. He was a pretty good teacher and explained everything real well. I just had a hard time using the alphabet instead of numbers. I did notice one thing he did that seemed kind of weird, though. He walked around the room and talked, but the strange thing was this little nervous twitch he had. What he would do was roll his class ring round his finger. It seemed innocent, but I believe he might have had ulterior motives. You see, most of the girls in the class wore miniskirts which left little for the imagination. It could have made a single young teacher a little frustrated. Anyway, he would drop that class ring right in front of one of those girls. None of the boys ever tried to pick it up for him either. I believe he may have been trying to get himself a free look. He was personable, though, and Jacob and I got to talking to him after class on a regular basis. The one thing I really liked was his car. He had a maroon 1967 GTO. It was a sweet ride. I believe Jacob liked that car even more than I did. There is a lot more to tell you about than some old, boring algebra class….

The Rams basketball team was the best around. Coach Bradley led the team and was the best high school basketball coach ever. He had some incredible players, too; boys like Kevin Price, Donnie Freeman, Bruce Lynch, and Bubba Simmons. To beat the Rams—well there just ain't no way.

To be honest with you, my sophomore year started in 1970 but ended in May of 1971. I wonder whatever happened to all the "beautiful people" of that year. I expect some of the guys have their chest in their drawers and some of the girls just might resemble that, too. Oh where, oh where did all the wrinkles come from? I am being nice by just saying that much. Whatever happened to those who were considered to be leaders? Where is Bubba, Susan, Bruce, Ron, Huanne, Bob, and Letice? They were hot stuff in 1970 but are they hot in the twenty-first century? The most handsome that year was Hugh Steele and the most beautiful was Debbie Carswell. I ain't judging, just curious as to where they all are and what they are doing these days.

I haven't mentioned the Blue Rambler Band yet, have I? Up until this year, Mr. Rigney had been band director. He had one of the best bands around but someone up and stole him away from us. Mr. Paxton was the new director and I just don't see how he could hold a candle to Basil Rigney. He was known for his fits of rage and ability to throw stuff. I know the band was probably still pretty good but I was just interested in the Majorettes. From the sophomore class, there was Crystal, Roxanne, Debra, Kim, and Cheryl. All five of those girls were something else to look at, too.

As I wind this informative session down, I would like to reflect, as a typical sophomore. Now this ain't me always talking either, it might even be a girl's reflections. Daydreams may be a better way to describe what you are about to read...Let me just share a little insight from the 1970 Newton High Yearbook.....

MONDAY

I'm sorry but I was just thinking about the weekend...I really did love the ballgame...How many times did he call you this weekend?...I went to see *LOVE STORY* Saturday... Whose yard got rolled this weekend???...Monday morning blahs...I hate Mondays.

TUESDAY

It was a little better today...I need to go to Mr. Najjar's office...Where's the Student Council report??? Football practice in the rain...I just can't type...Only two days in the week and I am already sick of this week...Everything is Tuesday...

WEDNESDAY

What clubs meet today?...I need to get some things downtown but all the stores are closed...My report was due yesterday??? Do the girls have early practice today?...I just love those short fifth and sixth periods..3 down and 2 to go...

THURSDAY

May I have a ride to the ballgame??? Did you hear the announcement?...We're gonna have a pep rally tomorrow...I wish it were Friday...What was that we had for lunch?...I love you...3:15 bell...Thursday, come again...

FRIDAY

I'm so excited...I hope the rain stops for the game...
ROCKY WHO??? What time is the bus leaving for the
game?...Who's playing at the dance tonight?...Oh no, we
play Therrell tonight...64 to 12??? It doesn't seem like
homecoming without a queen and a court...Hang it up,
Rockdale, you just can't win...I just adore Fridays...I feel
like I just lived through a whole week of school...."Fizzix"
test Monday, but Mr. Croom...Thank goodness it's Friday...
Beat the Rams...Ain't no way...Friday's child is...A Newton
County Ram...We're from Newton, couldn't be prouder.

1970 was a very interesting year, but I had no idea that
in just a few months, my life would change forever.

Remember Donna? Here is what she wrote in my
annual.

Ricky,

*I have really enjoyed knowing you this past year.
You are really a great and beautiful guy. I've had some
outasight times with you. I hope you will never forget
me because I will never forget you. I hope you live the
best life has to offer because you deserve it.*

Love always,

Donna

NOT BAD FOR A SOPHOMORE FROM THE PECAN
GROVE, NOW IS IT?????....

CHAPTER 9

Reckless Driving or Reckless Disregard

I was telling you earlier about Jacob and his fast driving. He was no different than most of the other guys his age. He had a need for speed and some fetishes just have to be fed. Fast food just had not really taken off yet. The only two places around town that you could cruise through were the Cow Palace and Dairy Queen on the other end of Highway 278. As the cars came through, there were usually a dozen teenagers standing around with their girls and a cold brew in a paper cup. They would taunt about everyone who had a car that seemed anything like it was hot. They would scream things like, "Light 'em up," "Burn 'um, boy," or "Come on, let's see what it's got." That was more than most any of them could handle. Jacob would ease over the speed breaker and dump the clutch. The bystanders would watch the smoke show and comment on about every car. You might guess, the local cops kept these to places about as hot as the teenagers did. There were usually at least two fights a night at each place or somebody would get a little rowdy and somebody else would call the law on them. Every so often, the cops would get lucky and catch one of the hot rods lighting up the tires.

Most of us had spent time at one or the other of these places. Jacob had made some more friends by this time. He and I were still fairly close; we just didn't spend quite as much time together. Freddie Launders, Ricky Johnson, and Doug Bailey were a few of the guys. You heard of two of 'em once before; they helped paint the town, without success.

One night, Jacob was out and made a spin through the Cow Palace. He did what he had done many times before; he eased over the speed breaker and when the back tires cleared, he dumped the clutch. It was sweet from what I remember him telling me. This time was a little different.

The cops came into the parking lot just as Jacob rolled off the speed breaker. As he eased out of the parking lot, the cop lit him up. He ended up getting a ticket for reckless driving. The fine was a whopping $35. It might as well been $350 because he had no way of paying it, unless he told his folks and got the money from them. He knew what would happen if they found out, so he was not about to say a word. What do you think your folks would have said if it were you? I can here it now: "Mom, Dad, can we talk. Well, I kinda got a ticket." After they asked what for, the conversation would go downhill fast. You get the idea?

At any rate, Jacob had not mentioned getting a ticket until he had just about a week to pay it and he didn't know what to do. One day after algebra class, Jacob told me about the ticket. He said, "I thought about seeing if I could borrow the money from Mr. Chambers. What do you think about that?" I told him I didn't know if that was the right thing to do, but if he thought it was, there was no harm in asking. Mr. Chambers' class was just down from the auditorium so when I headed to the next class, I passed back through the auditorium and down the hall past the main office. All during the next class, I thought about the idea Jacob had to get the money and had kind of an uneasy feeling about it. It wasn't my decision, though.

The next day after algebra class, I saw Jake talking to Mr. Chambers. Later, he told me our algebra teacher had loaned him the money. I asked him how he would pay back the money. Jacob said, "We already got that worked out. I'll wash his car and wax it or give it a tune up or something. It won't be a big deal." That sounded really cool because it seemed like Mr. Chambers might be a little cooler than I thought. Plus, he had that nice '67 GTO; now, that could work out pretty well. After that, I didn't think much more about our conversation and never mentioned it again.

Like I was saying, it seemed like Jacob spent more time with his newfound friends than the boys from the Pecan Grove. You've got to remember, though, we had already been through a lot together. It scared me a little bit because these new friends seemed to have no problem with breaking the law and doing stuff I would never think about. I don't remember the names other than those I already told you about. I do remember several of them had dropped out of school and a couple had already had brushes with the law. I heard about petty thefts and talk of more serious things. I don't think it ever went that far, though.

Before you knew it, hunting season had rolled around again and all of the boys enjoyed jumpin' rabbit or deer. I know Brent and his daddy did a lot of deer hunting. I enjoyed hunting, too, but I enjoyed riding my Honda 175 even a little more. I had it fixed after the wreck and it was as good as new. About every day after school, I would drink my Coke, eat my vanilla wafers with peanut butter, and head out on my Honda. Nothing changed much either. I usually rode through the trailer park and turned out onto East End Road. Some of us had even made some paths down to the Alcovy River and there the road was a little washed out, but it took you right to a nice clearing. It was the spot where a good many

111

people fished. Brent's daddy, John, had dropped some set hooks up and down the river. (Set hooks were a gallon jug with cord and a hook with chicken liver on it.) He would tie a small rope around the handle of the jug and tie it to a tree next to the bank. I had found 'em all when Brent and I were walking the river bank, so I would check 'em every once in a while. What I am trying to say here is we could always find something to do and sometimes, we would just run up on each other on the road or around the river. It really was not that unusual. That is why what I experienced later this day seemed pretty normal.

I did my usual after I got off the bus at about 3:45 in the afternoon. Mama had my Coke in the freezer so when I opened it, it was froze just enough to make it something like a Mr. Freezy. She had me five vanilla wafers with peanut butter for my snack. I threw my books on my bed and sat down at the kitchen table for my snack. Fifteen minutes later, I got my helmet and an extra one and headed out, out the driveway, down the side of the road, and then I crossed over to the Trailer Park. I piddled around a little that day in the park, talked with Jim Thompson and then turned right on East End Road. The Mallorys and Bishops were the only two families on that end of the road. Tim Mallory was Brent's age and we had gotten to know each other. He had a sister, Melanie, who was a couple of years older than me. I always thought she was pretty cute, too. Their mom had a Beauty Shop attached to the house. I guess thirty or forty-five minutes had passed and I headed back in the other direction.

This one-lane dirt road could get really dusty when it was dry and slicker than owl crap when it was wet. I remember, it was dry this particular day. When I came up to the curve and started toward the railroad road tracks, something a little strange happened. There was a big red-clay bank right at the tracks like they cut through it to put

112

the tracks down. Anyway, Jacob jumped down off the bank right in front of my motorcycle. He 'bout scared me to death, because he also had his shotgun in his hand.

Well, I shut down my bike and stopped. I not only saw Jacob but also his tag-a-long, Johnny. I asked Jacob what was going on and he told me he had just been through the woods to see what he might roust up. It seemed like Johnny was really aggravating him. Jacob asked me if I would let Johnny go with me. I agreed and we both pulled our helmets on tight and off in the wild blue yonder we went. After a few minutes, we had headed back toward the Mallory home and got just across the creek bridge right at the exit of the trailer park. We had to get off the road because a car was coming in the other direction. When it passed, I was surprised to see who it was. As the car went by, I threw up my hand and waved. Johnny asked me, "Who was that?"

I said to him, "Now that is strange."

"Why?" Johnny responded.

I told him, "That was Thomas Chambers our algebra teacher. I wonder what he is doing out here."

Johnny and I rode up the road and turned around to head back to the river. We pulled off on the little road just past the creek and headed down about forty or fifty feet. I shut off the bike and we pulled off our helmets. I reached in my windbreaker and offered Johnny a fresh rum-soaked cigar. Just as I reached in my pocket to get my small box of wooden matches, we heard a shotgun blast and it seemed fairly close and made me 'bout jump out of my boots. As I struck the match and offered Johnny a light, I said, "Wonder what they got. Maybe somebody just got 'em a deer, but it did sound like a shotgun; could have just been a rabbit."

He didn't say much; we just puffed on our cigars and tried to act like we were grown. We walked on down to the river and headed down the edge of the bank. We had to be careful because there were some places still slick. If we had fallen in that river, somebody would be draggin' it with hooks to find us the next day. After a while, we headed back and got on the motorcycle and went on to the house. I went on in and watched a little television while Mama was finishing up supper.

After we ate supper, I went to my room, closed the door, and did my homework. I thought very little about the day's events. It didn't seem much different than most other days in the life of a fifteen-year-old boy. I did wonder how Jacob faired on his little hunting expedition. I knew I would see him at school the next day and he would let me know then.

CHAPTER 10

What Really Happened?

The halls of Newton County High School were wide but always very crowded. The walls were that old, ugly mint green color and the ceilings had asbestos with what looked like millions of strings compacted together. The main halls ran to either end of the school. In one direction was the gym, in the other, the auditorium and lunch room. The other main hall led down the steps to the vocational wing.

As I was coming out of homeroom that next morning, I ran smack dab into Jacob headed down the hall. He stopped and seemed a little frazzled. He said, "I just wanted to let you know, Mr. Chambers gave me his car yesterday."

"GAVE IT TO YOU?"

"Yeah," he replied, "I took him to the airport; he said he had enough and was leaving town. When I turned to leave, he told me not to look back. He would mail me the title to the car."

Something was terribly wrong but I had no idea what it could be. I just felt queezy and my stomach was in a knot. As I was headed to my vocational ag class, I met Freddie right at the steps that led to the next wing. I said to him, "Have you talked with Jacob?"

He told me he had and that something didn't seem right. The stories that he had told us were totally different. Freddie told me he had seen Jacob in the GTO the night before and that he had hidden the car behind the Auction Bard at the corner of Jackson Highway and Starsville Road....Now, I was very confused.

I went on to my classes and throughout the rest of the day, I wondered what was going on. Then I heard the most disturbing news I had heard all day. Jacob had been called to the counselor's office where he was met by the investigator for the Newton County Sheriff's Office. Buddy Allgood was the only investigator they had at the time. I had heard about him; he had a reputation for being tough and didn't put up with any crap. I am not sure if people were scared of him but there was a feared respect. There probably was very little interviewing done there in the counselor's office.

James Otter was the Sheriff and most every adult in the county knew him personally. He was the epitome of a Southern Sheriff, with the Stetson hat, cowboy boots, and the western clothes. Somehow or another he must have found out Mr. Chambers was not at school. I am sure the administration suspected something since there was no substitute filling in. Anyway, Jacob's stories were already falling apart and somewhere in the midst of all the lies that had been told was a spattering of the truth. The investigator must have known there was much more to the story than what had been told up to this point. Jacob was handcuffed, put in the back of the deputy's car, and taken to the Newton County Jail. Just before the end of the day, the word that Jacob was hauled away was all over the school. By the time it got to me, I had begun to think that something unthinkable could have happened. I couldn't say for sure, but I just felt like Mr. Chambers was not going to be found alive.

I got home that afternoon and found Brent. He had heard about what happened to Jacob at school but that was all he knew. The talk in the neighborhood couldn't be quieted. I knew Jacob's parents must have been going through pure hell. Brent and I tried to put all the pieces together. Here was what we knew for sure: First of all, Jacob had lied. Mr. Chambers had not gotten on any airplane and left town. We knew Jacob did not get the car and hide because it was given to him. I knew Jacob had his shotgun the day before and we heard a shotgun blast that afternoon. I also remembered Johnny and me getting off the road to let Mr. Chambers down the dirt road. There must have been some sort of accident and Jacob was just too scared to tell. The day seemed to be getting real dark, real quick. The two of us figured we had better go home and see what our folks had heard.

Mama and Daddy were genuinely concerned and didn't quite know how to take what could be happening. They let Blue and Larue know they cared and were there for them if needed. There was a lot of praying during the next twelve hours. I just lay in bed that night and cried for a while and prayed for a while. This kind of thing just didn't happen to a fifteen-year-old boy from the Pecan Grove. We had seen an awful lot up unto this point, but never anything this serious, or what seemed this serious. I didn't sleep too well that night and knew I couldn't go to school the next day. Mama and Daddy agreed it would be too tough until all this could be resolved. We all needed answers and only had speculations.

When you think it couldn't get much worse, it usually does. By the next afternoon, the true story had come out. It seemed as though Jacob had been interrogated for hours before he finally broke. I'm sure it was like a dam of emotions let loose for him. The information we got came in pieces but this first bit was almost more than any of us could handle. We were told Jacob had admitted to killing Mr. Chambers. The information that unfolded over the next few hours was like putting a puzzle together. This puzzle, however, was the most horrid of any. It was hard to fathom, my friend and confidant was being charged with capital murder. I felt sick, confused, and literally scared to death. This had to be a nightmare; I would wake up and none of this would be true. What else could happen?? How was Jacob?? What would Blue and Larue do?? How was Johnny gonna handle all this?? How could I ever go back to that school and go by Mr. Chambers' room??

Not one of those questions could get an immediate answer. All of us, our neighborhood, and the families from the Pecan Grove had to support our own no matter how terrible it seemed. During those times, covered dishes for the mourning and fresh cut flowers for the bereaved were not uncommon, but what could we do for this family? None of us knew because we were all in shock. All of our folks had seen the mischief and rowdiness from the Pecan Grove boys. They had wiped our snotty noses, bandaged bloody knees, and even gave a cold drink when we were famished. We had all...grown up within shoutin' distance. We had laughed together, cried together, and celebrated together. Together we would get through this nightmare. And a nightmare it was.

The very shotgun blast Johnny and I had heard the day before as we lit up those old rum-flavored cigars was the fatal finish. That was the sound of Jacob's shotgun as it struck Mr. Chambers' head. I can't imagine what went through Jacob's mind during the next few minutes. What would he do? How could he explain? Who would believe him? He had to have panicked. There is no way he could have been thinking rationally. It was a struggle, and the gun went off. I was sure it happened that way. When he stood up and looked around, with blood spattered everywhere, a lifeless body just lying there, the word "reasonable" is just not in your vocabulary at the time.

Humpty Dumpty sat on the wall...Humpty Dumpty had a great fall....All the king's horses and all the king's men... Couldn't put Humpy Dumpty back together again....

Was that the case here?
Could we ever reach normalcy again?
WOULD JACOB BE OK?!!!!!!!!!!!!

CHAPTER 11

What Could Happen Next?

The very next day, after we had received the news that Jacob would be charged with murder, we all needed answers. Blue and Larue felt like they needed to see where all this happened. All that we knew so far was that Jacob had shot Mr. Chambers in the head and the body had been moved away from where everything went down. We all talked and agreed to park the car at the railroad tracks and walk until we could see something. I was not sure how good of an idea that was but because all of us were caught up in a whirlwind of despair, it seemed to be the right thing to do at the time.

They picked me up in the old brown Ford station wagon. As we backed out of the driveway, headed down Johnson Highway, and turned left on East End Road, I started replaying the events of that tragic day. I could remember turning my motorcycle around in the Mallory's driveway. When we passed the exit of the trailer park, I remembered pulling off the road to let Mr. Chambers by. I could almost see the look on his face, now that was spooky. Then I saw the little road where Johnny and I were when we heard the shot. About two minutes later, we were pulling up to the very spot where Jacob let Johnny get on my motorcycle.

We got out of the car and opened up the break in the fence. It was the same break we boys had used many a time

121

before to enjoy our freedom in the old Studebaker truck. We all slowly walked into the edge of the pasture and just stood for a minute. You could see where several vehicles had been in and out. We figured if we followed the tracks, it would take us to the scene of the crime. Just a day earlier, the place was swarming with cops and the coroner. I felt a huge lump in my throat but I did my best to stay calm. This was a somber time much like walking from the hearse to the gravesite after someone you really loved had died. The slow walk seemed to take forever and none of us could hardly bear the pain. Jacob's mama was hurtin' bad; this was bone of her bone and flesh of her flesh, her oldest boy. Blue was torn up, too. He was trying to be strong, but he was so overcome with everything that had gone on he just stared and tried to hold back the flood of tears that could have erupted any minute. Johnny was walking real quiet with crocodile tears running down his ruddy face.

We finally came to the place where you could tell there had been a good bit of activity. The broom sage was wallowed out like cars had turned around and people had been stirring around. It was about twenty-five yards from the creek then trickled down the edge of the woods. We all started inspecting the area with a fine-tooth comb. Johnny screamed, "I think I found it!"

We all walked over and saw a hunk of salt and pepper hair lodged in the dirt. I about freaked out. This had to be the place it all happened. Upon further inspection, we could see what appeared to be blood that had soaked into the old brown dirt just beneath the trampled vegetation. As we stood there, very few words were spoken; it was like all of us came to the point of understanding this was real and somehow we had to begin to deal with it. After five minutes or so, we found our way back to the car. There was an uncanny silence until we pulled back into the Hartleys' driveway.

Blue pulled up behind the house. I just got out and said, "I'll see y'all tomorrow."

I did go back to school and things did get back to normal, as much as they could anyway. There were just a few months left in the school year, and as normal, I was more concerned about extracurricular activities than I was academics. That meant another year in summer school if I planned on making my pass. This one would be a lot different, though. Not every weekend would be filled with fun. I would get my first car. I would go on my first single date. The thing that made this summer most different was that I would spend at least two Sunday afternoons a month at the old dilapidated county jail.

I will never forget the first time I went to see Jacob. As we walked in, there were smells I had never encountered before. It was a mixture of odors, the musty smell of an old brick and steel building would have been enough. It was kind of like a men's locker room that hadn't been cleaned good for twenty years and somebody tried to mask the odor with Pine Sol. I really can't describe it so you could get the full impact. We went around the dispatch room through a steel door and up some stairs. We saw prisoners who had been charged with about anything; we just never stopped to talk with them. The toilets and showers were out in the open; there was no privacy at all. Jacob was in the back of a "bull pen" with several other men. We just stood right outside his cell and talked to him. It was hard for me to think of stuff to talk about so I did a lot of listening. We did talk a little about his lawyer and a trial that would come sometime in the near future.

Jacob's folks intended on hiring the best lawyer around. They knew Paul Cook because his family owned all the land behind us. You might remember the old black sharecroppers. Well, they had looked after the Cook property. It was well known around town that Paul Cook was the best criminal lawyer around. There were all sorts of stories about this defense attorney. The story goes he killed one man in a boating accident and shot another one. Not one day did he spend in jail. You hear all sorts of stuff but there ain't no way of proving any of it. All I can say is he had a lot of experience with the criminal element. His son, Kirby, hadn't been out of law school long and was assigned to help with the case. At any rate, they all got crossed up and the Hartleys hired another lawyer out of Conyers. I heard the Cooks kept my friend from the electric chair, though.

Jacob stayed in the county jail about a year before the trial. The day before the trial, they took the deal. It would have been real tough to stand before twelve jurors and prove his innocence. That old courthouse had haunting memories of men who had gone to trial before Jacob's case ever came up. There had been several get the death penalty right there in the same courtroom.

As an eighteen-year-old man, Jacob received a life sentence in the state penitentiary. When he was sent off, I didn't know when, or if, I would see him again for a long time.

All the times we had spent together were now just memories. We couldn't talk about paintin' the town, eatin' pizza sandwiches at the Cow Palace, or even romancing. His girlfriend, Dinah, did stand with him during the whole process and even visited the state pen. She finally had to go on with her life, without Jacob.

As bad as it all was, at least life wasn't over for either of us. The years to come were a mystery for us but hope was around the corner for at least one of us....

CHAPTER 12

The Class Of '73

You have good days…smiles and rainbows and roses and Fridays…and bad days… tears and dark clouds and thorns and Mondays…but they all balance out in the end. This was how many felt even now as the Class of '73 was about to enter the old dingy halls of Newton County High School. This should be the most exciting year of a teenager's life. I could recollect memories of all the cool stuff we had done in the past year. A cherry bomb in a toilet does more damage than some would have realized…Detention for smoking in the bathroom had not been the end of the world. Sneaking a hug or even a kiss before you went to that dreaded English literature class was not so bad either. A cold beer, a pack of Salem cigarettes, and listening to Grand Funk Railroad on an eight track was a small highlight in our lives.

There was one thing for sure, Jacob Hartley would never darken the doors of this school again. Instead, he was in deep South Georgia in one of the most violent prisons in the state, at least for now anyway. Reidsville had a reputation and it was not for being the summer camp for troubled youth. It was dirty. It was violent, and it was tough. That dreaded place was where my friend called home. He probably lived in some six-by-eight room with gray concrete block walls and dark gray metal bars. He should have had his senior picture on page nineteen of the Rams yearbook. He was supposed to be between Brenda Harris and Debra Hayes. That was not reality and thoughts like that should be neatly tucked away in the recesses of my mind.

A lot of things had happened since April of '71 and since Jacob was sent to prison. It was not all gloom and doom, either. I had already seen my sixteenth and seventeenth birthdays. I had been involved in some serious romances and some not so serious ones. My first car had been bought and sold. You know, the first car is mighty nice to you but sometimes it is just a clunker. Mine was a 1964 Mercury Comet, solid white with a little six-cylinder engine that purred like a kitten.

The only thing was I didn't want something that purred; I preferred a tiger in the tank. I was able to convince my daddy I needed a nicer car for my senior year. We looked around and found several possibilities. A fellow who worked for the city had a '67 Chevy Camaro for sale. It was white with black stripes and was really sweet. Daddy did not like that idea. Then I found a '66 Chevy Impala, red with bucket seats and a four-speed. As you might guess, that one did not meet his fancy either. The third one was a charm. Barry Lane worked in a body shop his father owned. He decided to sell his 1969 Ford Torino GT. At one time, it had been a green metal flake car, but when he decided to sell it, he painted it orange and put a black vinyl top on it. It was a pretty hot car. Barry had built the 390 engine and put a set of headers on it. It was not long until I had picked up one of Jacob's old pastimes. Street racing was not only challenging but it was one of those things that gave you a serious adrenalin rush.

Back at NCHS, rumors were still circulating as to why the murder had taken place. Teenage investigation does not always prove to be the most accurate of crime solving. The teens involved do think they are the final voice, however. The most widespread story was as follows: Mr. Chambers was a pervert and he made advances toward Jacob. Jacob Hartley was a real man and there was not gonna be any other man try and grab or grope him. As a result of this improper advance, a struggle ensued and the shotgun went off. After that, Hartley panicked and well, as some would say, the rest is history. Some even said there was an accomplice, but I don't believe that is true. After all, I was no more than 200 yards away from where it all happened. Anyway, there was no way this story would ever die. Too many people had their take on the April day. The problem was since there was no trial, most of the stories were just that—stories. I never had the guts to just ask Jacob exactly how it all came down.

I had quite a few newfound friends and had even begun to think about what I might want to do when I graduated. Terry Manning and Wayne Shropshire had move into Alcovy Trailer Park. Their dads were working on the new interstate that would go all the way to Augusta. It was called Interstate 20. I was seriously dating a girl over on the west end of the county. Her folks had a shoe store downtown and also owned a moving business. Belinda Harris was a junior and had grabbed my heart and squeezed it. I just knew we would end up married when she got out of school. Belinda was a real cute girl with blonde hair and blue eyes. It evidently was not meant to be; we broke up before graduation, but continued to communicate through a mutual friend.

I worked at Ramsey Furniture Company most of my senior year. My friend Biff Hutchinson and I had some real experiences delivering furniture. Biff's dad had been the principal at E.L. Ficquett, before his premature death. His mom had been one of my fourth-grade teachers. Biff could do impressions of Sam and his dad, the owners of the family business; he sounded just like them. While off from the store, we did not share exactly the same interests. I had begun to become very interested in emergency medicine

Rick Darby

and I knew in 1973 Newton County would have its own ambulance service and the funeral home would get out of the emergency services. Because I thought I would like to work on an ambulance, I was able to volunteer at Caldwell and Cowan Funeral Home on Wednesday and Sunday afternoon. I never answered one ambulance call, but I did get to watch some embalming and move some bodies from the old cold stainless-steel embalming table into the casket after they had been dressed and made ready for viewing. It was a pretty weird job for a high school senior.

The first time I ever touched a dead body was when I was seventeen years old. They were very stiff and very cold. I would think of Mr. Chambers lying in that creek bed after Jacob had rolled him down the hill and covered his body with pine straw. I wondered what it was like touching a lifeless body that you had just snuffed out. What was going through his head while complicating his crime? I did think of that day every once in a while when I was watching the blood drain from the lifeless corpse and smelling the formaldehyde as it entered the arteries. Maybe it was what had happened that drew me to this occupation I had started to enjoy.

Before I knew it, my high school days were coming to an end. It was already April again. All I could do was think back to that hellish day. After two years, things had gotten a lot better, but I figured memories would fade with time. A teenage boy should not have to think about a murder that one of his best friends committed. There was good news, though; Jacob's mom had told some of us he was working on getting his GED and would be able to study a trade. She said he was going to try Auto-body repair.

I had ordered all of my invitations, my cap and gown, and our 1973 Newton Rams yearbook. We had over three hundred seniors graduating, so we would march onto the football field for that final act as students at NCHS. As the

128

time drew nearer and nearer, I got more excited. This would end a chapter and begin a new life. I had already planned to move out of the Pecan Grove on my eighteenth birthday. I was lining up my first full-time job at Newton County Ambulance Service. Everything seemed to be going quite well.

Finally, that day came, high school graduation. I snuck me a small bottle of Jack Daniels into the vocational wing classroom that was doubling as a dressing room for boys where were to get ready for the big night. I shared the liquor with several of my friends. We finished off the bottle and hid it in a trash can at the front of the classroom. Almost immediately, we started eating Certs breath mints like candy. As we all walked out to the field to find our seats, I remembered once again, Jacob would not graduate with his class. He would not enjoy a senior trip or in my case, a senior keg. If he had any idea how special this night could have been, would he have chosen another path?

On that hot, humid first Friday of June 1973, three hundred others and I walked onto the platform and received a piece of paper we had worked for at least twelve years. As the ceremony ended, we all stood, took off our caps, and simultaneously slung them in the air with a shout. It was over and we would go our separate ways.

It was 9:00 p.m., 2100 hours at Reidsville State Prison, and time for a head count. I would never regret the friends I made in the Grove or during the past four years at Newton County High School. There was one thing I knew I could never do, that was take back days, or say it never happened.

With particular certainty, as I left that field in June of 1973, I felt Jacob Hartley and I would have another day before we died. That insight was not from my finite wisdom, but from an infinite source, a source I would learn to depend on more and more.

129

About the Author

Rick Darby is a veteran police officer and an ordained minister. He currently serves as the police chief in Cornelia, Georgia. He has had the opportunity to teach over 5000 law enforcement officers, both locally and internationally. Rick has written feature articles for local newspapers and law enforcement training curricula. His passion for people has allowed him to appear on local, national, and international radio and television. He has also worked with troubled youth and taught drug education in public schools.

Rick and his wife, Debbie, live in Commerce, Georgia and have four children and four beautiful grandchildren. They enjoy spending time with their family and working outdoors. Rick has enjoyed telling stories for many years. He has the ability to write in such a way that you feel as though you are listening to one of his many stories as he tells it. His desire is to make you reminisce about the better days in your lives.

During the past several years, he has begun to develop thoughts and ideas concerning future books. Please watch for more of his work in the near future.

Printed in the United States
51852LVS00001B/334-342